the Day
and
the Hour

Finally

Lynn Andrew

The Day and the Hour: Finally

First published in 2020 by
Sorek Valley Books
sorekvalleybooks.com

ISBN 978-0-578-66507-8 (soft cover)

Scripture citations are paraphrases by the author
based on the American Standard Version of 1901.

All characters are fictional.

Composed in OpenOffice.org Writer.

Introduction

S he wants to believe that Earl Clark, the man she loves, will not be separated from her by the act of God she believes is bound to occur this morning. Yes, Leila persists in this desperate hope. Might he possibly come back to her before it is too late?

Yet she feels he has already, in some mysterious way, returned to her, a feeling that lingers from a vivid dream last night. Immediately after waking she wrote down high points lest it all fade from memory too quickly. Yesterday she had concluded that the case was closed, and she had tried to resign herself to the heart-break of losing him, but hope reasserted itself overnight.

The hope persists this morning in spite of a daunting perspective that loomed up as she spoke with Earl's father by phone yesterday evening. What she heard from him forced her to see Earl Clark in startling similitude to Samson of the Bible. This was not a complete surprise. She had noticed a shadowy suggestion of the Samson-and-Delilah story in her relationship with Earl; but when that gave her the notion to write a drama based on the classic story, casting the two of them in the leading roles,[1] she had thought of the play simply as an exercise of her playwriting side-line. Now she wonders if she had written it with an unconscious motive to explore the Samson in him—and the Delilah in her.

Leila had been aware that her role in the government,[2] which put her in a position of power over him, could be compared to Delilah's ironic domination of Samson. But as often as such thoughts occurred, she renewed her determination to never allow herself to become as extreme as Delilah was. Now that she has come into this new information from Earl's father, which corre-lates astonishingly well with the biblical hero, she has to wonder: could it be that Earl singled her out only because she bears some

---

1. As things turned out, the scheduled opening performance was deferred until next week; so it will likely never be performed.
2. Ms. Labaki is the chief executive officer at the local branch of the Federal Services Administration.

resemblance to Delilah? Had he revealed his secrets to her because she pressured him as Delilah had relentlessly pressured Samson to reveal the secret of his strength? In spite of her intentions—and no doubt his too—had their unfolding lives inexorably revealed them in those roles? According to the Bible, Delilah lived in "the valley of Sorek." Curiously, Leila lives there too, because the greater area in which this town is located is called that.

When Leila wrote the play, she understood the reason for the hand of God being upon Samson of old, for the biblical account makes that clear.[1] Could it be that the hand of God was upon Delilah of old too? Without her doing what she did, Samson would not have brought down the Philistine temple, an act that advanced (and culminated) his mission. That being true, could it be that the hand of God directed and moved the heart of Delilah as well?

Leila would not have thought much of this a few days ago, but now she is beginning to know the ways of God. This has helped her bear the irony of her role. She believes there may be a redeeming reason if the romance has a sad ending—though it could not be as sad as what happened to Samson, the tragic irony of which is almost too terrible for the reader to bear (and we assume that Delilah did not know and did not have to bear it).

The stark notion of God moving and using people as he did Samson is a daunting thing, even a dangerous thing. But Leila has come under the protection of her Savior, and she can face such hard truths without harm. She possesses a comforting trust that enjoys allowing God his sovereignty. Soon the dream of life will be over, and she will have no fear of seeing her Savior face to face. In fact, since her dream last night she feels that she already has seen him and has even received gifts from him.

---

1. The angel of the Lord appeared to the woman and said to her, "Listen: though you have been barren, you will conceive and bear a son. Now take care: I ask you to drink no wine or strong drink and eat nothing considered unclean; for, yes, you will conceive and bear a son but no razor shall come upon his head, for the child will be a Nazirite to God from birth, and he will begin to save Israel out of the hand of the Philistines. (Judges 13:3-5)

Introduction

Now to the main issue. This is the long-awaited day, and soon its fateful hour, 8:00 AM here or 16:00 UTC, will be upon us. This day and hour has been known for exactly one week. Last Sunday morning the world woke to the undeniable prophecy of it, though naturally it was widely denied. It informed us of a date that had heretofore been a divine secret; and now we know exactly the day and the hour of what is expected to be the Rapture—or translation —of the living church from earth to heaven.

The prospect of this antecedent to the second coming of Christ is mentioned in Scriptures written by the apostle Paul in which he anticipates the Savior calling living believers to heaven as well as resurrecting those who have gone on before. We may assume its purpose is to further prepare this group to participate in his kingdom, that triumphant millennial age when world government will rest upon the shoulders of God incarnate—the very Jesus Christ whose birth in the flesh of this world is not to be found on our calendar because our calendar begins with his humble birth and marks the days and years and millennia to his coming in glory.

The Scriptures leave no doubt that people left behind after the Rapture will witness severe pains which the earth must endure to make it fit for the new age. The reforms during that period of tribulation involve hardships that will change the minds of God's own skeptical children. Then after great tribulation the earth will give birth to the glories of Christ's kingdom, starting with his universally expected Second Advent which every eye will behold.

So if the church's translation takes place this morning, it will be an isolated event almost without warning (which distinguishes it from the main events of the Second Coming and its earth-shaking prelude). Though the likelihood of the Rapture being distinct from the Second Coming has been doubted by theologians and Bible teachers, it has been on the world's mind. The idea of people literally vanishing was so intriguing that it became the subject of countless enactments in literature, cinema, and failed predictions. But now with this evidence that the real thing is about to occur, Bible interpreters are facing a rare moment of existential truth.

The Day and the Hour: Finally

This is virtual heresy to several sorts of people. That some believers are worthy to escape the tribulation (and the horrors involved such as wars, famine, and disease) merely by confession of faith is far from the doctrine of salvation by suffering. And it never was considered quite fair even by those advocating grace when they fail to find the Rapture in Scripture. Yet the words of Jesus himself[1] have never met a more satisfactory interpretation.

Where does Earl Clark fit in? He is not a vocal disbeliever, but neither does he belong to the church. He is not ignorant about the claims of Christians, but something holds him back from joining the ranks of believers who anticipate the Rapture.

This past week has been a tumultuous time for Clark. He came close to being arrested for his involvement in an effort to shield his community from having to endure an oppressive intrusion on the part of the federal government.[2] Leila, in complying with an FBI stipulation, has placed him under the surveillance of her patrol officers lest he escape before his arraignment. She did this in a compromise agreement with the authorities in order to allow him a few additional days of freedom.

Unfortunately, Earl escaped yesterday afternoon. He slipped away and sought refuge in the city with an old girlfriend, Dr. Carmen Hayrab; and that's where he stayed last night. The city police, knowing his whereabouts, are guarding the entrances to the building. They have known since yesterday evening which apartment he is in, but they must wait for the arrest warrant to be issued this morning, enabling them to enter uninvited and take him at gunpoint. As far as they are concerned, this is for a crime he committed last night in which he struck, knocked unconscious, and handcuffed an officer who was attempting to arrest him.

---

1. "Because you have kept my word and persevered, I will keep you from the hour of trial that is coming on all the world, to try those who dwell upon the earth. Hold fast to what you have. When I come it will be quickly." (Revelation 3:10)

2. Known as the Reorganization, it brings pervasive surveillance and autonomous deterrent mechanisms to every street, building, and household as a means of preventing criminal behavior, which is broadly defined as anything that might bring discomfort to another living being or institution or transgresses the international, federal, state, and local codes of correctness.

Introduction

Leila knows these details. She has gotten police reports—in part from Earl's father who is an officer in the department. Indeed, she is the one who, after his disappearance yesterday afternoon, gave the police their instructions to search for him.

But she can do nothing to release Earl from the consequences of this latest crime. It would look hopeless to anyone else, but Leila believes it is possible that he will muscle his way through the barriers and break free of any restraint they attempt to put on him. Somehow, she hopes, he will find a way back to her. However, the time is very short, and the city is far away.

It appears that Mr. Clark is indecisive about his loyalties, does it not? Yes, that puts it mildly as you well know if you have been with us during the week. But can we blame him? You might point out that he could have picked a girl who was not employed by the "enemy." Samson picked a Philistine woman. If love sprouts up in a dangerous place and subsequent difficulties overwhelm, a likely reaction is to push back against Cupid's prank.

Not that Earl is blameless, but his faults are few compared to the seemingly endless list of his admirable qualities. The fault that has gotten him into his current predicament is his casual attitude toward authority, particularly when it comes in the form of law-enforcement officers and even more particularly when they are attempting to arrest him. Like Samson, he treats them as a joke.

Pastor Adam Murphy, who is also prominent in this story, is a friend of Earl's and happens to be one of the preachers in this town who received the Rapture announcement a week ago.[1] This past week was full of surprises and setbacks for the pastor. He is in a different frame of mind now compared to last Sunday. He began with a determination to reach as many people as he possibly could—that is to urge them to turn to the Savior and escape the calamities that he was confident would be coming soon to the world. Now he is worn down and disappointed. Yesterday was particularly hard on him. Certain events challenged his way of

---

1. So did a million or so others throughout the world, most if not all of whom are subscribers to the doctrine of the pretribulation Rapture.

explaining what life is and how it all came to be. He is no longer confident that he conveyed the whole truth in his teaching. More days and hours would be needed for that, but sadly his career as a preacher appears to be finished.

Because there are various kinds of belief, the world has reacted to the Rapture announcement in numerous ways. On one hand is the wide-eyed belief of those who see God at work every-where. On the other hand is the stubborn assertion that God never intervenes in human affairs or at least not dramatically. On neither hand are the uninformed unbelievers and the defiant dis-believers—those whose personal convictions are absent or acci-dental. Some worship idols or false gods while believing nothing or nonsense. Some worship Satan and other celebrities, not real-izing that devils believe and tremble.

But alert servants of Satan who have not been lulled into pas-sive acceptance of official denials would naturally attempt to reap some return from the Rapture. For example, we know about the stadium in Shanghai, China which is full of disabled unfortunates who are locked in together with a few able-bodied Christians. The authorities who concocted this scheme couldn't discount the real-ity of the Rapture dreams even though their respect for Christ was limited to seeing his kingdom as a serious rival to theirs. Because they knew nothing of the often-slow migration of sinful souls toward the Light of life, they thought they had an opportunity to be rid of some of their more costly invalids; they presumed that one Christian became two whenever there was contact with a needy person. They were partly right, but rarely does it happen so casually and never so reliably. (Those authorities had been taught the opposite in order to ensure their diligence in isolating follow-ers of Jesus from the rest of the population.)

Pastor Murphy has one final task set before him. A number of people are wanting to be baptized, or so he was told—or thought he was told. (The source of the information, which I will not take space to summarize here, was very strange indeed.) Although he has questions about what he was told, he plans to be there, at the

Introduction

Beach House on the lake (which currently is Earl Clark's residence and where Clark would be today if he had not skipped town).

The only other dwelling located on the bay at the north end of the lake is owned by Ken and Karen Martin. The Martins[1] also own the Beach House. Earl rents it from them. Ken and Earl are good friends though communication between them became limited as Ken's dementia progressed. Karen thinks the world of Earl, and it will be interesting to see how that plays out today. She follows Earl's lead in discounting the Rapture and has not been a faithful church member since Ken's condition made socializing difficult. Still, Ken is a firm believer in the Savior, and all indications are that he experienced the Rapture dream himself—making him the only layman who got the news first hand as far as we know.

The Martin Construction Company, owned by Ken and Karen, was the general contractor several years ago when they built the gym up on the hill overlooking the downtown area. Known as the Fitness Center, the gym is a government franchise which Earl Clark operates and keeps open weekday mornings before he reports to his regular job as a reporter with the local paper located down on the waterfront. Next to the Fitness Center is the new multi-story Federal Services Administration (FSA) building where Leila oversees upwards of two hundred employees.[2] Formerly, the main building of the goldmine occupied that hilltop spot exactly where the FSA building now stands.[3]

Today the town is smaller and less prosperous than it was a hundred years ago. Many of the buildings date from that era. You can stand on the parking lot in front of the FSA building and view the whole downtown area with its old brick buildings. It consists

---

1. Editor's note: It should say *those particular* Martins, for there are other Martins in town. The lode of gold which built the town was discovered by one Joseph Martin, Ken Martin's great-great grandfather.

2. Perhaps that should be past tense because she has put in her resignation, effective Monday. -*Ed*

3. What began as a short exploratory tunnel down by the creek became a substantial gold-mining operation with many shafts and tunnels within the hill.

of only three blocks along the lakefront and essentially two blocks inland. You get a great view of the mountains east of the lake from there too.

The view from Ms. Labaki's offices on the top floor is breathtaking on a clear day. You see the bay where Earl's Beach House is located just a short distance to the north, on your left. You don't see it from the ground, but up on Leila's floor you see over the treetops, and the Beach House is clearly visible, including Earl's shop where be builds his sailboats. To get there by road you have to go to the highway located on the west side of the hill, drive north and then east on Mountain Highway and turn right when you come to Beach House Road. If you were to go by water it would be much shorter, but you can't get there by walking along the beach because there is no bridge across the creek.[1]

The farthest-north building on the waterfront is the Lakeview Restaurant. Beyond that is Gold Creek and the spit of land at its mouth which narrows the entrance to the bay. A trail starts near the Lakeview parking lot and goes parallel to the creek on its south side. About a quarter mile away from and above the trail, Creek Street follows the same general course. Pastor Murphy's church, Grace Bible Church, is located a short distance up from the Lakeview on Creek Street. Beyond that are some residential streets crossing Creek Street, one of which, Deer Drive, is where Leila Labaki's apartment building (which she owns) is located.

Earl has made his beach available to Murphy for baptisms, no doubt because Earl Clark and Adam Murphy are best friends and not because he cares to promote Christian baptism. On the other hand, the Beach house is somewhat of a community treasure, having been built by Joe Martin, the founder of the town, and one of his sons. So Earl would not turn down any reasonable request to use his beach and dock. Moreover he shares his fleet of small sailboats with the community. He built them for that purpose, and he offers free sailing lessons Saturday afternoons, one of which Leila participated in yesterday.

---

1. In fact the creek is fenced off.

Introduction

Today I hope to get an update on what I've called the "Council of Seven" for lack of a proper title.[1] These are the men behind the committees that mastermind the world. So you will not think I made this up, I will tell you where I got my information. We first learned about these kingpins by the chance connection I mentioned in *Tuesday*. I did some imaginative filling-in of details, of course, but the basic biographical information came from Rabbi Avi who, for a short time, was a reluctant member. What I have not told you is that Evelyn and I spent the remainder of Thursday evening and well into Friday morning working on this. In fact, Sunday's[2] last soliloquy at the end of *Tuesday*, chapter one, she dictated to her secretary as we sat in my parlor discussing these things. You see, Evelyn already knew about Sunday and his council. I believe she knew more about their spiritual connections than they did. So what she contributed to chapter one in *The Day and the Hour: Tuesday* is technically fictional but substance lies behind it. Whatever appears here in *Finally* adding to that will have to come from another source, and I have one in mind. Always there are rumors as to whether such powers exist and where the antichrist fits in. Sunday, the dictator over this council, would be a natural for that role when the time comes.

Who is Evelyn? She is a State Department employee—one who travels the world, not a sedentary bureaucrat—currently on loan to the FSA and being used to advise community leaders in advance of the Reorganization.[3] What reason she had to visit our obscure town is a rather long tale, but it may be condensed to one statement by saying that she is a friend of Adam Murphy's and came here to be baptized. She, along with Leila and a number of other people, were baptized by Murphy here yesterday afternoon.

---

1. The number on the committee had been reduced to six when Rabbi Avi disappeared and was further reduced to five by another casualty as they met in Rome on Tuesday.

2. The committee members never used their real names, and even their codenames were changed with some frequency. Lately they have adopted the names of the days of the week (reminiscent of G. K. Chesterton's *The Man Who Was Thursday*), Sunday being the leader's current handle.

3. See footnote 2 on page 6.

The Day and the Hour: Finally

Earl had encountered Evelyn on Thursday morning in Herne, a town not far from here, where he had gone to sit in on a meeting she had scheduled for the benefit of the residents there—to give them advance information about the Reorganization and to encourage them to support it. That was her mandate and what she was supposed to be doing, but it turned out that she was advising them about how to effectively forestall the implementation of the dreadful thing. In a conversation with her after the meeting, Earl discovered that she had been forced into the liaison role against her will. No doubt she was conscripted on account of the exceptional attractiveness of her person, which would help her sway the sort of men she would most likely find opposing the Reorganization.

Evelyn took special interest in Earl when she learned that he lived here in this town, and unfortunately Earl misread her intentions. He was surprised when he discovered that her primary interest was not him but that she wanted to be baptized by Adam Murphy, whom she had not seen since her high school days in Appleton, Wisconsin where they had worked together on the school newspaper.

When Evelyn got here she called on the FSA executive, of course, and the two of them became friends immediately. Evelyn waited until the evening service at Murphy's church to surprise him and request baptism, which she did. They scheduled it for Saturday when Evelyn and her entourage would return for the occasion.

By then Leila had decided to be baptized too. She was not a Christian believer when she first met Evelyn, but by Thursday evening she had became one, not by anyone's direct influence, but Evelyn did have something to do with it—and so did certain words in the newspaper that Earl had written, oddly enough.

On Friday Leila sent her testimony to all her FSA employees, and a number of them responded favorably and appeared at Grace Bible Church Friday evening. By Saturday they and others had joined the baptism party, which had become a crowd

Introduction

descending on Earl's beach as he and Leila returned from her sailing lesson. Earl, being a nonparticipant in the religious proceedings, found himself virtually a prisoner in his own shop as his house had been overrun by people using his bathrooms and changing into bathing suits.

Evelyn noticed this and stepped into Earl's shop and tried to convince him to join them. Her words brought no good result, for shortly after that, as everyone watched Leila being immersed in the lake by the pastor, Earl quietly slipped out, hustled up to his garage, and escaped in his vintage T-Bird Roadster by outwitting Leila's officers who failed to keep him in sight.

A question that needs to be answered at this point is why more baptizing needs to be done today when so much of it was done yesterday. Today's candidates are short-time believers, some having understood only since yesterday that the truth of life is found in a Person, not a creed; and they want to do whatever they can in the little time we have left to show their sincerity and appreciation to Jesus for covering their moral deficits with his perfection. If Christ offered his blood to secure a righteous standing with God for them, they want to testify that they consider themselves dead to their old life and alive to their new life in him by the symbolism of being buried in the water then presently rising to new life. I know this is their belief because I sat in on some of Felix's lectures.

Without Felix, who showed up here on Monday with the intent of committing a crime, there would be little need for last-minute baptizing. Why he came here and how he turned from his wicked ways is a story that would not fit in these introductory pages even in summary, so if you don't know about this, I encourage you to go back and read the other books.

By the way, without Felix we would know nothing about the miracles that happened in the Shanghai stadium on Friday.

Philip and Pamela Evans are long-time residents and two of the sincerest Christians I know. They own Evans Hardware, which they had decided to transfer to their employees. But when they convened a meeting yesterday morning to announce that intention, they discovered that they had invested far more of the Spirit of Christ in their employees than they realized; and they were astonished to find that none of them wanted to be left behind to run the store by themselves and that they had, in fact, conspired to join the Evanses in the Rapture. That accounted for quite a number of the baptisms yesterday.

Then yesterday afternoon Pamela intentionally got herself booked into the jail by publicly pressing Sgt. Al Cypher to consider his liability of going to hell. Her purpose was not to convince Cypher of anything—which would be a futile effort—but to make him angry enough to lock her up, thus giving her an opportunity to preach to the inmates. Philip told me when I spoke to him last night that her effort bore fruit—which you may already know.

This jail, I must tell you, is located on the ground floor of the FSA building, and, as with everything in that building, the amenities are first class. In fact the official and apt designation of the facility is Detention Suites.

I salute Pamela Evans for what she has done. Those men, who up until Friday were vagrants living in the woods, are being held in Detention Suites pending transfer to a Reorganization laboratory for experiments. No one here was in favor of this, but it is quite within the diabolical spirit of the Reorganization.

There is more you must know about Al Cypher. As warden of Detention Suites, he has not been kept very busy by that duty. In fact, this is the first time the jail has had occupants. His other duty is being the security officer for the FSA building itself, which is not a demanding assignment either. Apparently he spends most of his time dreaming about his boss and plotting to supplant Earl Clark in her affections. I'm certain it was Cypher who sent evidence of Earl's Reorganization-resistance committee to the FBI.

Harold Foster is another stalwart of the faith, but his wife, Harrietta, is something else, though she professes to be among the saints (and I hope she never reads this, and I have reason to believe that she won't—more on that later). Harold had quite a time early in the week when his boss, Neva, made a desperate attempt to keep from losing him with his technical expertise in a mammoth software project that was nearing completion. Though she lives in the city where Harold's place of employment was located, I managed to obtain a contact number for her, and will try to reach her and get the rest of her story.

For today's record, I'm particularly interested in learning how each of the many characters in this story are feeling now that the fateful day has arrived—and what they are doing about it. As all roads once led to Rome, so I will try to have as many of them as possible appear here in this final volume.

In addition to Adam Murphy, a number of other clergyfolk made their marks last week. Chief among them is Adam's older brother, Aaron Murphy, pastor at Our Lady of the Lake Catholic church. Adam, believing that he had but one final opportunity to sway his brother, met with him on Thursday but to no avail. Fr. Murphy has not joined the Rapture believers and neither has the Church embraced that relatively novel concept, though she has acknowledged the phenomenon of the Rapture dreams and proposed other explanations.

Neither does Rev. Kirby Amill, who is employed at the Presbyterian church here, accept the Rapture doctrine. Though at one time he began to take interest in premillennial theology, he went back to the comfort of not having to deal with controversial aspects of the Bible's teaching about the return of Christ and what happens after that.

Russell Tarr, pastor at Kingdom Hall, supplements his income working at the hardware store. He is ambivalent about the Rapture as well as many other things. At one point he called on Pastor Murphy and announced that he was considering revolting and breaking with Watchtower. But he could not quite let go of the credit towards a blissful destiny that he believed he had accumulated.

Rev. Veronica Sweet had to work hard continually to keep her congregation, which consisted of people with a special interest in heaven. Hers is a virtual church dealing in virtual reality which she creates for her parishioners—for a donation.

I must include Laura here, though she is not professional clergy (far from it) because Laura and Veronica became close friends this past week. They are a pair of opposites who differ so much they fascinate one another. Veronica is well educated with multiple degrees and has done extensive religious studies. Laura I presume finished high school. She is a simple soul and knows virtually nothing about religion. Veronica will tell you that Laura receives more knowledge of the mind of Christ in fifteen minutes than most Christians acquire in a lifetime. I have known Veronica for some time, and that statement comes from a humanist who practices religion for profit and as a psychological experiment and has little genuine respect for people who say they believe in heaven. She thought she knew every religious type, but Laura astonished her. I don't know where Veronica stands at this point, but according to what she says no one could be more confident and thrilled about the Rapture than Laura is.

The last clergyperson, if I may stretch the category to call her that—and she really isn't anymore—is Clio Endoor who lives next door to Veronica Sweet. Clio began the week hating Christians, especially true believers, for she was the leader of a witches coven. Did I mention that there were a number of miracles this past week? By Thursday Clio was teaching the Bible to new believers. It turned out that she absorbed history like a sponge absorbs dew. She began reading the Bible at Genesis and very soon became saturated with the Old Testament and became qualified to teach it by her enthusiasm and her preparations. So I will say she is now serving as a clergyperson without abusing the category.

Incidentally, I think it's clever that all of these professional clergy, including Adam Murphy and a couple of others, live on a two-block stretch of Parson Street. Another thing you may have noticed is that most of their names contain double letters, Adam Murphy being an exception. Your guess is as good as mine for what that means, if it means anything.

Introduction

Other prominent members of Adam Murphy's Grace Bible Church include Brother Ned, a founding member, who I suspect will remain a member until the day he dies. Leonard and Lina are regulars too, but they have not had a high profile this past week, so I would not venture a guess as to where where they stand.

Simon, another member of the Grace congregation, is the one we all know who tries to be wise beyond his ability. He works at the hardware store but was not present when the other employees testified that they had adopted the faith of their employer and were eager to make the trip to heaven.

Doris is one who tenaciously holds to her doctrines but whose capacity for them was one-hundred-percent filled long ago. She regarded the Rapture day-and-hour announcement as impossible and a heresy to be shunned. As far as I know she has not changed, but we will see.

Lucinda is a nice lady who, I found out from Alice Murphy (the pastor's wife), was not pleased to hear the Rapture announcement. You can read what she said to Pastor Murphy in *Tuesday.* I will not repeat it here. She is a woman who speaks her mind. I think she would be a better fit in the Catholic church. But I have to give her credit for doing the research on the Nicolaitans.

I have encountered Connie on a few occasions.[1] Her initial reaction, as she expressed it during that famous evening service at Grace Bible Church a week ago, went something like, "It might be better to wait and see before making too much of it. People hate us when we appear to think we're superior to them in some way. That doesn't accomplish anything."

If Connie speaks boldly in a large group, she can be deadly in a small group, policing everyone's ideas and setting them straight immediately. I know she confused Laura on the matter of obeying the law vs. taking her daughter out of school to go visit her parents. Even Pastor Murphy avoids getting into a discussion with Connie, I understand.

---

1. Some of these names I have changed and have omitted surnames because they are actually composites of more than one person.

17

The Day and the Hour: Finally

Archie is another one who spoke up in that Sunday evening service when the question "What shall we do?" was being discussed. "I'm not sure we should do anything different," he said. "We've been living our lives every day, knowing he could return at any hour. So now we know he will return at a certain hour—or at least we're pretty sure he will. But I don't see why that should make a big difference in what we do."

What would you call that?

On Friday Adam Murphy visited Archie, who is a retired architect with many unusual designs to his credit, and got a primer on how designers make use of evolution. Archie was about to see his book on the subject go into print.

Philip told me Archie appeared in his dream last night, one of the select group of men who were being prepared to work on the rebuilding of this town. But was his dream a true prophecy?

You remember Ellen White. Who can forget that transformation at her daughter's wedding?—the wedding that didn't happen, I mean because her daughter didn't show up. It was truly astonishing. It might have been her salvation. What do you think? And what about her husband John? Does he get a free pass for putting up with her? If not, and Ellen goes without him, he misses ... well, who knows? You never know about families from the outside.

What about that fireman and his wife?—and their little brats? I spoke with Harold after he and Philip called on them. He has some hope for Ed.

And what do you make of that rear admiral among us, Mr. Smart? If the Rapture does happen, there will be surprises—surprises either way, I'm sure.

Maud, one of my neighbors, is a sad case if there ever was one. She has had a rough time in life, has no family to speak of, and she really was not interested in joining the Rapture. Will her wish be granted? Lately she has been associating with two young Mormon ladies who have blessed her with their presence and entertained her with readings and songs. They deserve a great deal of credit for braving the horrible smells in that house.

Introduction

Now Richard and Richelle I know very well, and I have pretty well decided what will happen to them. They are faithful attendees of Adam Murphy's church, which should count for something. Richelle is such an agreeable person! I think she would be fine with it either way.

Ahuva—dear Ahuva. She has been utterly transformed these last couple of days after Mark decided he would be her friend. It's truly amazing what love can do. Ahuva was not the prettiest girl in the high school while Mark was quite popular in spite of his being a forthright Christian. He saw something he liked in Ahuva that apparently no one else saw. Personally I think she has much going for her. Her father is a Jew but not her mother who I have heard is a Christian—or had professed to be at one time.

What about Jake? Don't ask me about Jake. He aligns himself with Grace Bible Church though he is not a member nor is he a faithful attender. He is Claudia's significant guy, but frankly I think she would not mind too much if he disappeared. It would solve one problem for her or perhaps two. The man is his own boss and he knows this town pretty well, having bought and sold real estate here for most of his life. That's all I can say.

Both Harold and Harrietta are afraid that their teenage son, Homer, has sold his ticket to heaven by joining the Catholic church. Why should that matter? was my question. He did it in order to play on the baseball team. This was Claudia's idea. When she took over sponsorship of the Autumn League team, she made a rule that its members must be boys and members of the Church.

Earl Clark manages the team, by the way. The final game of the season took place here yesterday. Homer pitched the entire game and did very well, but still our Leaders lost to the Herne team. Homer's girlfriend, Victoria Martin, pitched the entire game for the Hornets—in fact all their players were girls except the catcher. It was a close game, and I believe we would have won if the manager had not taken out our best hitter, Asher Cypher, simply to spite Asher's father. So, in a way, it was a contest between Earl Clark and Al Cypher.

The Day and the Hour: Finally

Speaking of tickets, we have two sets of travel-lottery winners who are not here, but I hope to get updates from them by tonight and include them in the proper sequence. Here is the background:

Lucy and Larry Link and their dog Larry Jr. left yesterday morning for the Great City (which encompasses the location of ancient Babylon). You may not know, if you have gotten this book through retro-sphere publishing, that the Great City has become the hub of the business and financial world in an astonishingly short span of time. The original plan was for it to mimic and possibly exceed the attractive aspects of every other modern city not only in its trade and commerce but also in recreation and as a resort destination. Though all of the infrastructure has not yet been completed, there was announced suddenly last week a lottery to bring in hundreds of thousands of tourists. So Larry and Lucy Link and their dog are on the other side of the world right now. Yesterday they departed for the Great City on a ticket Larry "won" in the lottery.

The other lottery winners are Ernie and his wife Enid who won a six-day vacation cruise to Alaska on a ship which is scheduled to return to Bellingham today.

Dr. Soren Foster and his wife Sylvia have been in town all week, but I have heard little from them other than a few details from their archaeological tour of Babylon. I understand that Adam Murphy visited them on Monday with the intent of making sure they understood the Rapture issue. While they are members of his church, their attendance has not been regular, partly because they travel quite a bit. Soren has retired from his medical profession. He's the brother of Harold Foster, and Soren has been sore at Harold over a—well you can read about it in *Friday* where Claudia gets Harold's story from Harrietta over lunch at Claudia's mansion. They impress me as the type of people who would not be much concerned about the Rapture or anything of that nature. Soren is a lifelong resident, but I must give Sylvia credit for her interest in the history of this town—not that that has anything to do with the issue at hand.

"And I know also that a passion, dominating or tyrannical, invading the whole man and subjugating all his faculties to its own unique end, may conduct him whom it spurs and drives, into all sorts of adventures, to the brink of unfathomable dangers, to the limits of folly, and madness, and death."
–Joseph Conrad

The Day and the Hour: Finally

Who can count the dust of Jacob
or number the fourth part of Israel?
Let me die the death of the righteous,
and let my last end be like his!

Numbers 23:10

Whoever seeks to gain his life will lose it,
but whoever loses his life will preserve it.

Luke 17:33

Everyone who has left houses or brothers or sisters or father
or mother or children or lands for my name's sake will
receive a hundredfold and will inherit eternal life.

Matthew 19:29

The hour has come to wake from sleep.
Salvation is nearer now than when we first believed.
The night is far gone; the day is at hand.
Romans 13:11-12

Chapter One

The Day is at Hand

*L*eila woke to the great disappointment of being in her bedroom—but it was early. She closed her eyes and tried to drift back into the dream. Parts of it were still vivid while she lay between sleeping and waking, but as the hour of her normal rising approached, even those scenes began to fade. She sat up and quickly jotted down a few words about things she could still remember, but that did nothing to restore the mystery and delight of being there. When she tried to enter into it again from her sketchy recollection, she found she was uncertain about how the various elements fit together.

She gave up trying to reconstruct the dream and lay back down. Faint light of the autumn morning filtered through the curtains. She listened to the noisy birds outside her door. They must be intent on bringing up the sun, she thought, for a lesser task would not merit so much effort.

6:00 AM

With nowhere to go and no desire to partake of worldly nourishment, Leila is uncertain about whether to get up and dress or stay in bed. She decides on the former for no particular reason, makes the bed, showers, and puts on clothes typical of what she would wear if she were going to the office.

This doesn't feel right. I wish I could remember what I was wearing in heaven.

She looks through everything in her closets and finally decides on wearing the clothes she wore yesterday to her sailing lesson with Earl.

The Day and the Hour: Finally

As she opens the bedroom curtains, the glass door frames a layered scene. The ornamental garden, beginning a few yards away, has pathways adorned with a layer of blue gravel that appeared yesterday. The green lawn beyond the garden shrubs glistens, damp with dew. Stately evergreens, towering above all, dominate the distance; yet she thinks the nearer trees contribute the nobler part of the scene, their fall-colored leaves of red, yellow, and amber looking pastel in the early light—leaves soon to be lost will leave the limbs bare.

She goes wandering about the apartment, entering each room as if to bid it farewell in whatever the future holds for this town. In the living room she stands for a minute before each of the paintings. One in particular holds her gaze and brings a tear to her eye. These pictures are reminders of that momentous time when unexpected circumstances kept her much longer than she had planned to stay at Lolomi Lodge in the mountain valley. It became a turning point in her career: it caused her to leave the national headquarters and step down to manage the Administration in this small town. She chose these mountain scenes for reminders, but none of them had ever made her cry. Now this one in particular is affecting her strangely. Is she sorrowful because she will be leaving this painting behind?

It was in the dream! That very mountain!

She lingers and stares at it, trying to remember the part of the dream where a similar but grander lodge faced that mountain scene. People she knew were there. They had become her family and she was introduced to children who had been waiting for her. She tries, but she cannot remember Earl being in that scene.

In the kitchen she finds Earl's gray hat with the yellow bill, the one he left when he came for dinner Wednesday evening. She picks it up and puts it on, but it is too large. She takes it off and holds it to her bosom, carrying it with her as she goes from room to room. Bidding everything goodbye to an uncertain end is proving to be too difficult, so she looks for something that needs to be put in its place or something to straighten up.

24

The Day is at Hand

Leila's thoughts have returned to Earl, if ever they left him, and she decides it will do no harm to get an update. Returning to the bedroom, she picks up her phone and checks the mail. Hourly reports from her local surveillance team are there, but they are informative only in that Earl's location is still presumed to be in the city. They are reporting no new information from city police.

7:00 AM

It is still possible that he might escape and come back just in time. If he were to get to his car, he would be hard to catch. Their rubber bullets and short-range patrol cars wouldn't stop him. Maybe that Carmen woman isn't truly his girlfriend. He won't be able to stay with her long without being arrested, anyway. Good thing I'm dressed. If he comes, it will be in a round-about way. He might leave his car behind Pastor Adam's church and take the trail. ...

Leila stops herself, realizing that she is engaging in unrealistic and wishful thinking. She remembers that she has already decided that the question is settled: he will not be joining her. She is not tempted to go back and review the reasoning on which she based that conclusion, for she is not sure there is a reason she can articulate, and the exercise would likely be futile and certainly painful. She does not want to discover that her conclusion cannot be wrong: hope never dies completely—not permanently.

Even if his spiritual condition won't allow him to go with me, he might come to say goodbye. ... No, I'm fantasizing again.

She is suspended between despair and some unearthly hope seeming to have emerged from last night's dream. She picks up her notes and tries once more to reconstruct it and this time succeeds in part. She remembers walking in a long corridor with Earl. And then she danced with him—or was it Jesus? Then....

That's it! We were in a wonderful lodge in the mountains, like Lolomi only more ... more heavenly. I know Earl loved Lolomi too even though it was only in his imagination. We talked about it Wednesday night when he was here. ... But the lodge in the

25

dream was larger and open to the fresh air. ... And I had children—and a baby!

She goes to the dining room and sits where she was sitting when Earl was there for dinner, when they talked about the ranch resembling the one in a book[1] they both had read. The memory of other things from that evening and the rift that ensued brings on a wave of regret and a feeling of disappointment.

It just didn't work out. ... But he was definitely there in one part of the dream.

Leila gasps. "Flo! Flo, how could I forget you?"

In her preoccupation with Earl, she forgot to find out whether Flo was prepared for the Rapture. Florence is here in town because Leila found her the job at the flower shop after Lolomi was shut down and the valley turned into a wilderness nature reserve. It was Florence's parents who owned the lodge and Florence who had lent her the book that captivated her imagination and led her to look for a place to live in the West.

Leila leans forward, spreads her arms on the table, bows her head, and pleads with her Lord on behalf of Flo; and the Spirit comforts her, letting her know that Flo is ready. They will meet again at Lolomi.

It is now close to the promised hour. During the past two days —since her rebirth in Christ—she often tried to imagine what it would be like when this hour drew near. She would be praying constantly, perhaps seeing visions of heaven, excited as never before in her life. She finds it is not that way at all: she is still attached to earth with her heart hurting for Earl now more than ever in spite of her repeated resolutions to let him go. To offset this, she determines to spend the last few minutes with her Bible.

Hebrews, she learned somewhere, is an important book, but it is not one with which she is familiar. She opens the Bible and turns to it, landing at the eleventh chapter where her eyes fall on *Samson*. She was unaware that he had a place in the New Testament. This fascinates her. He is listed along with other heroes of

---

1. *The Call of the Canyon,* by Zane Grey.

the faith: Abel, who offered the proper sacrifice; Enoch, who was translated before the flood; Noah, Abraham, Sarah, Isaac, Jacob, Joseph, Moses....

"Rahab the prostitute?"

> She did not perish with those who were disobedient because she had given friendly welcome to the Hebrew spies.

"I'm going to ask her about that!

Gideon, Barak, ... Samson! ... Jephthah, David, Samuel ... who through faith conquered kingdoms ... stopped the mouths of lions ... of whom the world was not worthy ... and apart from us they should not be made worthy."

The world was not worthy of them, yet they needed to be made worthy....

"How could that be? There's a mystery here."

While the fragmentary similarities between her Samson and Samson of the Bible were intriguing, she never before regarded them as being seriously significant. If anything, it warned her to be on guard against becoming a Delilah. She recognized the potential and saw the danger long before becoming actively involved in detaining Earl for his captors. Looking back, she sees the plot unfolding, casting her in the role she had wanted to avoid.

Yet hadn't she deliberately written the play to cast herself as Delilah and him as Samson? What made her decide to retell that story? At that time the answer seemed simple: it was a great story, and great stories needed to be told and retold over and over again. Could it be that all of life's experiences are based on stories being retold? How often it has been observed in patterns of history! Are there eternal scripts being replayed with variations on themes? If so, why? Because patterns are the very stuff of life? If so, the future might be read in the past: the resemblance between Earl and Samson could be significant.

"Who am I to make him worthy? He needs to believe the Scriptures!"

She decides to leave her Bible open and the door unlocked.

The Day and the Hour: Finally

*P*hilip woke with an aching neck from sleeping on the cot without a pillow. He tossed the tarp aside, stood up with a groan, and walked to the front of the store. Outside, the street was in dim daylight and deserted. He looked at the time; it was seven o'clock. He recalled coming to the store last night but could not remember exactly why he had done it. It now seemed rather foolish. He went back and put the cot away. Then he left the hardware store and drove home.

As soon as he arrived home he called Pamela. She told him again about the responses of the men last night, and he thanked the Lord for letting him suffer a little in support of what she did.

"How was your night? Were you able to sleep?"

"I did sleep. But I had a crazy dream."

"Was it about heaven?"

"I'm not sure what to make of it. How would I know if it was true?"

"I suppose it doesn't matter much now. We have only a few minutes to wait, and we'll know."

"Has Al Cypher come in yet?"

"No. He said not to expect him very early on Sunday morning. These are not his normal working hours. There are some eggs left, in case you want to have breakfast."

"I'm not hungry at all. I feel like I had breakfast already."

"The refrigerators in these suites are stocked with fruit and milk and yogurt, and there is cereal on the shelf—in case the prisoners need midnight snacks. But I'm not hungry either. I was praying when you called. I wish you were here and we could go together."

"Yeah, me too."

"Well, we'll soon be together in heaven. ... Phil? Are you still there?"

"I'm here. That dream is bothering me. It might be more complicated than we ever thought it would be."

"Heaven is complicated?"

"It might be. I'm sure there will be time for us; I'm just not sure it will be immediately."

The Day is at Hand

*H*arold Foster was glad to find Harrietta sleeping soundly when he opened his eyes, so he moved slowly and silently to avoid disturbing her, putting on a robe and being careful to make no sound as he left the bedroom.

He tiptoed to Hannah's room and managed to wake her and whisper his plan before she made noises: they would spend their last minutes together in the kitchen and not disturb the others. "If you decide to get dressed, be very, very quiet. Or you can stay in your pajamas and put on a robe if you like."

Hannah cooperated nicely. Within a few minutes she had joined her father in the kitchen where he had prepared the table for her with a peeled and sliced a banana.

"Mother is still sleeping," he told her quietly. "I think she got to bed very late, so we need to let her sleep. Do you think you can wake Holly quietly and have her come down to the kitchen too?"

"What about Homer?"

"He got home late and needs to sleep too."

Harold was confident that he would not leave his daughters behind, but he was uncertain about Harrietta and Homer and did not want them to witness the breakup of the family or be present during the tense moments leading up to eight o'clock. With the girls he knew he could maintain a prayerful attitude and a sub-missive if not fearless expectation. He was afraid that Harrietta would not be of the same mind and would make it difficult for all of them if she were present. As for Homer, he had no reason to believe that his son would accept an invitation to join them.

Hannah came back with Holly who sat down and said nothing. Harold brought another banana to the table.

"Will Jesus knock on the door?" Hannah whispered.

"No. It's not like that," said Holly.

"Shh. Whisper," Hannah reprimanded her. "What is it like?"

Holly breathed in Hanna's ear: "It's like what nobody knows."

Then after a few moments of silence Holly said,

"I don't like this, Dad. The whole family should be here."

"I agree, that's the way we would like it to be. But what would your mother prefer? Would she be happy to be waiting with us, or would she be a little nervous about it?"

"I see what you mean. She never really wanted to be part of it. But I didn't either, to tell the truth."

"I did," said Hannah. "Is Humphrey going too?"

They both looked to Harold for an answer.

"There is much we don't know," he said very seriously. "But we can talk to God about it. He's invited us to speak to him, which means there is a reason for prayer, and if there is a reason for it, it makes a difference. Go ahead and tell him what is on your heart."

"Can I tell him Humphrey would like being in heaven?"

"How do you know he would like being in heaven?" said Holly.

"Because I'll be there. Humphrey always likes to be where I am. Can I go up and get him, Daddy?"

"You can go up and bring him down and take him directly outside. Be very careful and don't make any sounds. Leave him outside when you come back in. You can let him in before we go."

Hannah got up from the table and tiptoed out of the kitchen.

Holly had said little, and she had not touched her banana. "This is very scary, you know," she said.

"Yes, it certainly is," answered her father.

"But you're not afraid, are you?"

"In a certain way I am."

"Because?"

"Because I lack faith? Yes. It seems to take more faith than is possible, doesn't it?"

"So you think it might not happen?"

"I don't want to say it in those words, but it comes to the same thing. It's unreal. It contradicts all our experience. And so little is given to us about preparation for it. Most of all I'm very surprised that we were given a week of warning. The warning itself was a miracle, but nothing like the miracle we face this morning."

Holly looked very serious. "Everyone says heaven is a wonderful place," she said.

"Do you doubt it?"

"I don't know. I've heard you say there's almost nothing in the Bible about heaven."

"Yes, but there's a lot about Jesus returning, resurrection of believers, and eternal life for us. I believe that's where we fit in, and there will be a place for us."

"Like what?"

"Jesus made some promises. Here is one of them from Matthew, chapter five:"

Blessed are the poor in spirit, for theirs is the kingdom of heaven.

"What if you're not poor in spirit? I don't buy that," she said. "You get to own heaven if you're afraid to do anything?"

"The two halves of that verse are in opposition," Harold replied. 'Poor in spirit' is like the opposite of possessing all the kingdom of God offers. So if you feel that your spirit cannot thrive in this world, the promise is that you will feel quite fulfilled in the next."

"I don't feel poor in spirit. I just am sad because I always thought it would be a blessing to have children."

"There's a promise for that too. The very next verse says,

Blessed are those who mourn, for they will be comforted.

"Jesus understands your disappointment and promises you it won't follow you in the future. The relationships we'll have in his kingdom will be more satisfactory than what we might have here."

"It's just hard to imagine," said Holly.

"Perhaps we shouldn't try to imagine it and instead meekly accept whatever God has prepared for us. Like in the next verse:

Blessed are the meek, for they will inherit the earth.

"What could we ever imagine that would fit that description?"

Hannah reappeared. Having taken Humphrey out quietly, she had come back without him, still tiptoeing silently.

"It's okay if God wants to leave Humphrey," she whispered.

Suddenly Harrietta appeared. She walked into the kitchen smiling, and she threw her arms around Harold from behind.

"Thank you," she said.

The Day and the Hour: Finally

Veronica Sweet was having a difficult time with herself this morning. She had slept fitfully and gotten up earlier than usual only to find that Valentine had preceded her. The girl had gotten dressed and was writing a letter for her mother to read after she was gone, and she made no secret of what she was doing. This upset Veronica.

Her initial reaction was surprise because she had almost forgotten that her daughter had talked about being born again. Surprise immediately gave way to fear that she had lost some part of Valentine who had come under the influence of her friend Emma and Emma's aunt Laura. The writing of this letter was evidence that Valentine had converted to their way of thinking. Veronica did not accept their way of thinking, and knowing her daughter, she knew there was nothing she could say that would bring her back. She reacted by adding anger to her fear. It was the anger that really upset her.

Veronica understood why she felt this way. It was not about what her daughter was doing or had done. It was about the fact that she had become angry, for if she were firm in her conviction that there would be no Rapture, she would have no fear; the hour would pass, Valentine would be embarrassed and apologize for going against her mother's advice, and the household would get back to normal.

Yes, Rev. Veronica Sweet was far from being certain about the position she took, but to admit that this radical thing was a possibility would be to admit that her rejection of the Bible as a relevant document was wrong. And that she could not do. But in fact, Veronica had carried on her unorthodox ministry knowing full well that she was wrong, for she was entirely motivated by a kind of rebellion.

"Can I go see Emma for a little while?" Valentine asked.

"No. Absolutely not!"

"Mom, please give your heart to Jesus. We will all be so happy, and we'll all go to heaven together!"

The Day is at Hand

Mark and Ahuva had agreed yesterday to use up the minutes remaining on their phones by sharing with each other the last minutes of their time on earth.

Ahuva woke Mark early this morning with a text message. She had been texting with her friend Ahuva in Jerusalem during the afternoon and evening there, which was after midnight and early morning here. They had been attempting to speculate about life in heaven, trying to find out what they believed they needed to know —basically who they would be with and what the relationships would be like.

Ahuva in Jerusalem did not have a boyfriend, while our Ahuva had Mark. Would everyone have a special friend in heaven? Would there be less difference between male and female there? Would some have more than one special somebody? Would Ahuva be Ahuva's best friend, or would Mark be her closest friend, or would both be special in different ways? The more they wrote about it the more questions they had.

She put some of these questions to Mark. She was tired for having been awake all night while Mark was not quite wide awake yet and had no answers. The questions would have been beyond him even had he been awake: they seemed to be the sort of things girls were always concerned about. But he recognized that there was something of importance even to him standing behind the questions.

Mark had begun rereading Ephesians last night. He had read the short epistle in the past, and each time he read it he was amazed to so see things he had not noticed before. So he came back to the epistle frequently. He had fallen asleep reading chapter four, which describes life in the body of Christ. He understood that the body of Christ was permanent, not to be dissolved in heaven. This morning it occurred to him that answers to Ahuva's questions could be right there. So before making voice contact with Ahuva he scanned through the verses, looking for words that would apply even in heaven. He found plenty.

The Day and the Hour: Finally

"Here's what it will be like," he told Ahuva. "In heaven there's one body and one Spirit, and Christ is the head from whom the whole body is joined and held together. As members of his body we each have a new self, created after the likeness of God in true righteousness and holiness, and we're eager to bear with one another in love, humility, and patience. Always speaking the truth in love, we grow up in every way into him, which makes the body grow so that it builds itself up in love. We are kind to one another, tenderhearted, and imitators of God as his beloved children, for we walk in love as Christ loved us and gave himself for us."

"Whoa. ... I should have talked to you first."

"As high as heaven is above the earth so are his thoughts above our thoughts."

"It's a huge makeover. Do you think we'll even recognize each other?"

"Of course we will. We'll still be who we are. We just get rid of all the stuff that causes us trouble now."

"Like being jealous?"

"What do you mean?"

"What if you meet someone you really like and you want to spend all your time with that person?"

"I wouldn't be in heaven if that's the way I was."

"Because it wouldn't be fair to the other person, right?"

"No, because I wouldn't be joined to the head of the body."

"Does that mean we want to spend all our time with Jesus?"

"I think so, but I think it's more than that. Don't we spend all our time with him now? It's just that we have trouble with the old nature. When we get rid of that, we'll really know what it's like to be joined to the head, and I think all our problems will be gone. In Jesus we want to be serving each other, not ourselves. Just like he showed us when he was on earth."

"Like, everything will be upside down from the way it is now."

"Don't you mean everything is upside down now?"

"Yes, I do. I'm learning so much. ... It didn't say anything about male and female. Do you think I could ever have children?"

34

"Jesus told us there will be no marriage in heaven."

"Could we have children anyway?"

"No, I don't think so."

"So we'll all be, like, unisex?"

"The Bible never calls God or angels 'its.' There must still be male and female. Also the New Testament speaks of the church as the bride of Christ."

"Like, everyone will be female because we're married to Christ? Are you sure?"

"No, it couldn't be quite like that. I wouldn't know how to be one. It would be someone else, not me."

"What does being the bride of Christ mean, then?"

"It's just another expression of how we all belong to him. We are his body too, so we can't be both his body and his wife. Neither one makes sense if you try to think of them literally. They both tell us how much we will depend on him. It's supposed to be that way now, actually. For some people I think it is. I'm looking forward to never doubting and always being aware of him."

"I'm glad you won't be female. In fact that would be awful."

"I can't imagine you being a boy, and I wouldn't want to try."

"But I thought sex exists for propagating the species, which is what my mother told me—she said never believe what they teach in school. So if women won't be having babies in heaven, what's the point?"

"I don't know, but I agree what we learned in school wasn't always true."

"What else could it be?"

"What else can we think of that men and women need each other for?"

"They dance sometimes. But that's just a mating ritual. Animals do it too."

"Really? All dancing?"

"Well, no, maybe not. I never learned to dance."

"If we dance in heaven, it won't be a mating ritual."

"Do you think there will be dancing in heaven?"

"There'll be music. It seems unnecessary to not allow dancing. But I wouldn't want to dance with another guy. And there will be singing. It wouldn't be heaven if it was all male voices."

"I wouldn't mind. No, I like female voices too, but not as much."

"You're fortunate. You'll love to listen to the voice of God."

"That doesn't seem fair at all. Maybe there'll be lady angels with beautiful voices. No, I'm sorry; that wouldn't be a substitute. You mean the voice of Jesus, I think, don't you?"

"Well, Jesus is God. He became a man and made a way for us to be like friends to him. Does that sound like an advantage for men? You would know better than I would."

"Why couldn't women be his friends?"

"You're right. I'm sure it means both.

"I know: fathers and mothers. But I won't have a father, will I? —because I don't think he believes in heaven."

"Could I be one for you?"

"No! Of course not! I need someone older. We both do, don't we?"

"Someone will adopt you, I'm sure. Maybe you could even choose your father."

"Do you think so? ... But I don't know. I might be too sad that my real father doesn't want to be there."

"Maybe you could adopt children, too."

"Do you think we could adopt children together? And have a family? Oh, wouldn't that be exciting, Mark? ... I'm sorry, the time has run out on your caller's account. If you would like to continue the call by transferring time from your account to your caller's account, please press one. ... Now enter the number of minutes you wish to transfer. You have two minutes remaining in your account. ... Thank you. Your caller will be notified. Stay on the line and we will attempt to reconnect your call."

"Mark, are you there?"

"I'm here, but we have less than a minute left."

"I don't know what to say. ... I love you, Mark."

"I love you, Ahuva. ... I'll see you in heaven."

"I'll ... see ... I'll see you in heaven."

Before I was aware of it, my desire had set me
among the chariots of my liberal people.
Song of Solomon 6:12

Chapter Two

The Escape

*E*arl Clark is awake but not dressed—barely awake enough to push the button on the coffee machine as he stands in Carmen's kitchen wearing only his underwear. He slept in—slept much later than is his habit—and is groggy for it. The night's sleep was not refreshing.

Carmen's bedroom door is still closed. He misses her—misses sleeping with her, which is why he is not dressed. He checks the clock again: 7:50. In ten minutes he will knock on her door, go in, and comfort her. He knows she will want him then.

Though she was always eager to give herself to him from their first date, Carmen was not essentially promiscuous. She was strongly attracted to Earl for his manly aspect. She wanted to bear a child by him, a baby who would be a superchild and grow up to change the course of the universe. Someday, it was her belief, the forces behind nature would not be denied, and he would give in. Meanwhile, she lived for weekends, working during the week at her dental practice.

This routine ended abruptly several weeks ago when Earl called to say he had made a commitment to perform in a play, and the Saturday rehearsals would make it difficult for him to continue seeing her regularly. She was relieved in a way. The drive to make him her mate—a mandate she had believed was in the stars —had gradually lost its aura of destiny. So it was not terribly difficult for her to accept this obstacle, and mating with Earl suddenly lost its urgency and inevitability. She decided she must begin looking elsewhere, but she had no enthusiasm for it and had not begun to do so.

The Day and the Hour: Finally

So, when Earl came knocking on her door yesterday afternoon after a long absence, it was a complete surprise. She had to make up her mind quickly. Had he contacted her ahead of time and asked for a date, she would have turned him down. But she could not refuse his plea for shelter. She decided she would have dinner with him but not invite him to spend the night in her apartment. However, after she helped him elude the police, she relented and let him stay because he needed a place to hide. She thought it would cause a terrible struggle within herself to make him sleep alone, but it did not.

Earl believes he will yet be in bed with her this morning, for such was his reasoned expectation when he lay down on the couch last night. He knew she believed in the Rapture, for they had talked about it. That is why, he thought, she had held out.

Regardless of her intellectual persuasion, it seems to him highly unlikely that she is in any danger of being included in a divine abduction. In a few minutes that will be made clear.

As Earl sips his coffee and waits to go in to her, he suddenly remembers that he is in a precarious position with respect to the law. He decides to get dressed in case there comes that unwelcome and perhaps inevitable knock on the door sooner than what he originally expected. It comes back to him now: leaving the hat behind last night was a big mistake.

Carmen thought her name was in it. If there's any competence on the squad at all, they'll have my location pinpointed. I wonder if Dad knows about my predicament. It won't be any surprise to him if he does.

Earl hurriedly puts on his shirt, pants, and shoes; then he goes to stand at the door to the patio. The expansive rooftop courtyard is one floor below. Various small structures are on it, one of which must be the entrance to an emergency stairway. As he drinks his coffee he studies the layout. He determines that a particular housing near the middle of the courtyard is the most likely candidate, which is confirmed when he spots a small *Exit* sign on it. But getting down to the courtyard from this level would be a problem.

The Escape

L ast night when Carmen asked Earl what he believed about the Rapture, she would have preferred to agree with his skeptical stance, but she could not. She was not a student of the Bible and had no theological basis for believing that the prophecy was what Christian believers said it was. She believed it simply because she saw no other way to understand how so many prophets could be in agreement. That was an inescapable fact, and it was altogether beyond anything nature could produce.

When Earl scoffed at her conclusion, she did not take offense, for she scoffed at it herself because it was not like her; she was not acting like her normal self when she accepted a doctrine straight out of a traditional religion. Whether it made sense or not would not have mattered because normally she would never have stepped beyond the security of her agnosticism long enough to consider whether it was true or not.

Indeed, something had undermined her agnostic fortress during the past week—or possibly an erosion of its foundation had begun earlier. Whatever the reason, she discovered a curiosity lurking within her that made her susceptible to considering the evidence on its own merit. When she asked why she had allowed sympathy for a Christian doctrine to gain such a strong foothold in her mind, the only thing she could put her finger on was that she had never disliked real Christians. She could always tell when she had one in her dental chair, and she loved having them.

This morning Carmen has been in and out of sleep for hours, sometimes dreaming of the numbers on the clock, sometimes waking, watching the minutes go by, and thinking: What if she should be taken along with the Christians? She would be painfully out of place. They had something that she lacked, and it made them confident of being at home in heaven.

They're not perfect either, but they have peace. It comes from being forgiven and made perfect in God's eyes by means of the blood shed by Jesus on the cross—so they tell me. Apparently, it works for them.

The Day and the Hour: Finally

This had never meant anything to Carmen before—as applying to her personally, that is. It makes her uncomfortable to be thinking about it now. In spite of that, she feels an attraction to the concept. Oddly, she is not bothered by doubts that Jesus lived and died and lived again.

Not much time is left. She hears Earl in the kitchen. She does not want to get out of bed and have to face him. She wishes she were sound asleep and pulls the covers over her head.

What ever possessed me to believe in this Rapture fantasy? ... Does my merely believing it mean I might be taken too? I can't deny ... I mean it would be foolish not to believe God does miracles. But ... is this me? I'm supposed to be agnostic! Oh, well. That was yesterday.

Now I'll have to reason this out on what little I know. Shedding his blood for sinners is what only an extremely loving God would do. Why would he be that way? ... Well, of course he would have to be that way because if his love were not that far above human love, he would not be God. All right, it might go somewhere. I could get interested in this. But if I'm not careful, next thing I know I'll be praying.

Sorry, Carmen, or whoever you are now, you cannot remain unmoved by that. If Jesus Christ bought you with his blood, who are you to resist? You would be throwing it back at him!

"Where did that thought come from?" she wonders aloud. "No, I would not—could not—do that."

How awful! Never, never would I reject his love. ... How could anyone?

Logically she has gotten into a corner with no escape. And as she admits that fact, she feels a surprising liking of being there. The complete absence of any displeasing emotion, like fear or resentment, is astonishing. The myriad consequences should she become a believer seem no more substantial than morning mist.

Carmen reaches out to her nightstand and takes up a pad of notepaper. She will leave a note for Earl, just in case. It had better be a quick note.

The Escape

*M*eanwhile, as the coffee brought on more clarity, Clark realized that his current escapade had reached a dead end, and, no, it was not the threat of the police.

Earl's desire to use Carmen had ended abruptly, and in its place grew a strong sensation that he was in the wrong place—not just that he was not in his proper place, which was obviously true. It was as though he had gone down a road using the wrong map, and he did not know what road he was on. Something had gone terribly wrong with the way he felt about being in her apartment. He stretched, swung his arms, and took another gulp of coffee.

Every few seconds Earl checked the clock. He had thought it would be easy to pass the time while the world waited with bated breath, but now he found himself disoriented, nervous, and per-spiring. Pressure was building to do something, to go somewhere, to escape while he could, but with no settled conviction of pur-pose, the clock claimed his attention and held him captive.

Yes, a new light was dawning: a renewed mind and a fresh spirit was coming upon Earl Clark. It would soon illuminate his true purpose; it had already shown him the petty wantonness of his plan of a few minutes ago. Indeed, he could not see a reason why he would have come here in his right mind. Who was Carmen that he should have come seeking comfort from her? Everything was wrong about it. As noted, the wrongness had nothing to do with the imminent danger of his being arrested; it was far worse than that. It was a feeling of having mishandled and broken some-thing very precious.

Earl looks into his empty coffee mug.

Was there something in there besides coffee?

He sets it down on the counter and peers out through the glass door. If there is any hope of restoring what has been lost, he must try to remember what it was!

The sun is not high enough to cast direct rays into the gardens of the courtyard, surrounded as it is by the towers of the building, but enough light is coming directly from the sky overhead to give an appearance of early morning. One of the gardens reminds him of the garden behind Leila's apartment building, and the answer comes to him in a woman's voice like that of Evelyn when she coached him on Thursday as they sat at the Garden Restaurant: *"She was in your thoughts last night, and she will never leave you."*

This prompts him to recall the dream last night in which he recounted Leila's virtues, and the details of it come pouring back. Grabbing up his mug again, he takes one step toward the coffee maker and stops.

It was't a dream!

He had been awake and had decided he must return to her immediately; but instead of getting up right then as he should have done, he let sleep steal his resolve.

As Earl stands frozen by the sudden realization that he let a good chance to undo his error slip by—and that it might have been his last opportunity—his mind comes fully awake and he grasps what the precious thing is that must be restored: Leila must know that he loves her; he must set her heart at ease.

The floor sways suddenly, and the coffeemaker skips on the counter. Earl looks at the kitchen clock.

8:00 AM

"An earthquake! That's what it was: an earthquake! They got warned of an earthquake, bless them!"

Earl goes to Carmen's bedroom door and knocks.

There is no answer.

"Are you all right?" he shouts.

No answer.

He knocks again and listens for the faintest sound.

There is no sound.

He opens the door to a smoky dampness and a strange odor. He steps in and looks about carefully. She is not there.

"Oops. ... It was more than an earthquake," he mutters, though not meaning it seriously.

The Escape

No, she wouldn't have been taken. She must have gone out for a walk while I was sleeping—probably didn't want to be here when the cops came. Why didn't I think of that?

The bedclothes are in place but carelessly arranged, which seems to indicate that she plans to return. He notices a piece of notepaper lying on the dusty floor with something written on it.

The doorbell rings.

Earl snatches up the note and tiptoes to the entryway. The hallway monitor is showing two husky police officers at the door. One of them has a key card in his hand, undoubtedly programmed to unlock the door. The other holds a large handgun.

Rushing back to the kitchen, Earl slides the glass door open and steps out onto the patio balcony.

Bam! Bam! Bam! Loud knocks assail the apartment door.

It is perhaps twelve feet down to the garden level, but there is no fire escape: evidently there is no means of getting down.

"Oh, yes there is!"

Rolled up and bound by a scarlet thread he finds a fire-escape ladder. Apparently Carmen put it there. He snaps the ties, and it flops down, unrolling its array of rungs. In a flash Earl has swung over the railing, scrambled down the ladder, and is running at top speed for the emergency exit near the center of the courtyard.

But scarcely has he crossed the garden area when the lawmen emerge from the apartment onto the balcony. Taking a stand there, the gun is aimed at him.

"Stop! Clark! Stop, in the name of the law!"

Earl Clark does not stop. He keeps running. Gunshots tell him he should be feeling the sting of bullets. Instead there comes a buzzing, humming chorus, and several large bees attack him.

It's a bee-bee gun.

Bee drones are darting, diving, and attempting to land on him, and one of them alights on the back of his neck. He reaches for it, plucks it off, and smashes it on the ground. Others are clutching his clothing, trying to poke their needles through to his skin. He brushes them off—the ones he can feel—while trying to maintain his stride. The door to the exit stairway is on the opposite side of the small structure, and as he slows to round the corner, two of the bees attack one side of his head simultaneously. He knocks them off, and they swoop back almost immediately. Another is clinging to his shirt in back where he cannot reach it, extending its needle into his flesh. He backs against the wall with a twist, crushing the mechanism, and it drops to the concrete.

Evidently at least one of the cops has come down the ladder, for he hears booted feet pounding on the garden path, their echoes clattering in the courtyard.

Clark's hand is on the exit door, pulling it open, but he feels another needle in his back. He must either let go of the door, allowing it to slam shut, or permit the bee to inject him with sedative. He tries to fling the door wide, but it is stiff, and his usual strength has waned. It opens partway then springs back immediately, yet he scrapes through, and in doing so dislodges the bee. The door slams shut behind him.

Down the stairway plunges fugitive Clark, chased by one of the mechanical bees. He takes a swipe at it and knocks it out of the air, damaging its wings. As he leaps to the first landing, he hears the door opening above.

"Stop! Clark! You're under arrest!"

Bang! Bang!—rubber bullets this time. One strikes him on the back, and it stings sharply.

Rounding the switchback at the landing, he leaps down, taking three steps at a time while the heavy boots come pounding after him, resounding loudly in the narrow stairwell.

Another landing and a third one fly by. He is far enough ahead now that they are unable to take another shot at him. He is thinking that if he can get down to the garage level before they emerge from the stairwell, there is a chance he will find his car close by and be inside it before they shoot again.

Flight after flight, the floor numbers go by. Floor **18** was the garden level where he started; he is now passing **10**, but he is out of breath and taking the steps only two at a time.

The Escape

Though Earl is ahead of them by three or four levels, he knows he must increase his lead. Apparently they are slowing too, for they sound farther away. Even so, once down and into the garage he will have very little time to reach his car, and he is not sure of its location relative to this stairwell. It could be some distance away, and if so the chances favor it not being in sight. It will take time for him to become oriented and find it.

Reaching the **P1** level, he bursts through the door and into the underground garage. Thinking it will increase his chance of escaping if he can find a way to barricade the door, he looks around for something to serve the purpose, but he finds nothing and wastes a few precious seconds.

Now, where's the T-bird? ... Ah, there!

Fortunately, the car is nearby, not fifty feet away. As he dashes toward it, the thundering of the boots in the stairwell increases. While standing beside the car and unlocking the door he notices a heavy chain lying on the concrete floor. His only means of escape has been shackled to a pillar.

The stairway door flies open. "Stop! Hands up—we'll shoot!" comes the cry from the angry law enforcers.

Earl crouches behind his car for shelter. From that location he sees the exit door he would be driving through, but obviously there is no possibility of removing the chain or breaking it, for he has not the strength of Samson.

Adjacent to the large exit door for vehicles is a small pedestrian doorway. The only remaining possibility of escape is through that door, and he will have to get there on foot.

A determined spirit has come upon Earl Clark. His mind is clear now. He distinctly remembers the dawning that came to him last night; the full awareness of it has rushed upon him. His life is worth nothing if he cannot reach Leila. He must make it very clear to her that he loves her. He must reach her before the authorities capture him, and after that they can do whatever they will with him. But he will make sure she understands what has been a mystery to her.

45

Unless she's gone.

Half running, half crawling, trying to stay out of their sight, Earl steals to the next car and the next.

Even if it was the Rapture ...

This method of movement is working; the noise of their footsteps has ceased. He dashes across an aisle, exposed briefly to their sight, and there is a shot and its echo, but it misses him.

... she might not have been taken.

The officers will have to be careful to avoid shooting the cars, which gives Earl an idea: he is almost as safe in front of a car as he is behind one—unless they send the bees again.

If I'm lucky, they used them all.

He must move fast now because they know his location, and they are pursuing him again on the run. Earl takes off, heading straight down the aisle for the exit door.

If she's still there, I'll get to her. ...

He knows his pursuers are unable to shoot while they run; he also knows they will stop and fire at him before he gets to the door. But what else can he do? He goes straight for it.

Somehow, I'll get to her.

A spray of shot stings his back as he reaches the door, and he plows into the exit, forcing it to fly open into daylight as another shot peppers his back with stinging beads.

If she isn't ...

Whether he is losing blood or not, he cannot tell. He suspects that he is, but he is not taking time to find out and does not care. The door swings shut behind him, providing a few seconds of shelter from the bullets.

God forgive me.

Up the ramp Earl Clark runs, panting heavily, and he reaches the street level without a plan and with no means of travel.

Now what?

A police car is there to greet him.

Earl has not the wind to go running down the street.

What good would that do anyway?

The Escape

It looks as though Earl Clark has failed in his desperate attempt to get home. Truly there was little possibility of it even if he had attempted to leave last night. No doubt he would have found his car chained to the pillar even then.

As his pursuers charge up the ramp behind him, he realizes there is nothing left to do but allow himself to be taken into the custody of the police.

Walking toward the police car with his hands up, Earl is letting them know he is surrendering, but a reflection on the windshield makes it impossible to see the officer inside. As he approaches the side of the car, the truth is revealed: through the side window it appears that no one is inside though the engine—a gasoline engine—is running. He quickly drops his hands, tries the door, and finds it unlocked. His pursuers, having seen him with his hands up and believing he has surrendered, stand a short distance away.

Before they realize what has happened, Earl has gotten into the driver's seat, pulled the door shut, and squealed away from the ramp.

Finding the siren and light controls, he blasts a path through traffic, sending vehicles ahead of him scurrying to the curb. With sirens wailing and warbling, Clark goes speeding down streets and careening around corners like a stunt driver in a chase movie or like a madman with no concern for his life.

Having attained the main arterial heading east, it is now a straight shot to the freeway. Traffic lights, responding to the signals sent by his car, are cooperating, holding cross traffic and allowing him to travel at high speed.

While weaving among city blocks, Earl had one close follower: an electric police car which had the ability to accelerate to high speeds in short distances, more than matching the performance of his gasoline-powered vehicle. However, that kind of driving causes a heavy drain on the battery, and his pursuer slowed and dropped out of the race. But now another one is on his tail; in the rear-view mirror he sees its bobbling lights not far behind.

The Day and the Hour: Finally

Nearing the freeway entrance, Earl has to slow down for cone-bounded curves and other obstacles in the vicinity of a construction project, which allows his more nimble pursuer to draw near. Being a smaller and lighter car, it rapidly closes in, bearing down on him from behind.

Rounding the last curve, Earl hits the brakes because a barricade blocks the road: a makeshift gate constructed especially for him. Police cars are stationed on both sides of it, their lights dancing in seeming delight at having cornered their quarry.

The barricade consists of a bar placed through the loops at the tops of two tall, weighted traffic tubes, preventing him from going ahead and leaving no room to maneuver. They have him trapped.

These guys are good.

Earl comes to a full stop at the bar. They will be adding the theft of the cruiser to the counts against him. An officer walks toward him as a loudspeaker on one of the cars blares an order:

"Shut off the engine, and get out of the car. You are under arrest!"

In answer, Earl presses the accelerator. The tires squeal, the hood of his car contacts the bar, and it slides back to the windshield. He floors the pedal, surging forward and dragging the heavy tubes, but he knows he will not get far in this condition, especially considering the incline immediately ahead.

The car that was pursuing him is still right there on his tail. With the pedal to the floor and the engine roaring in low gear, Earl has nearly reached the top of the hill when he cranks the steering wheel hard, sending his vehicle into a spin and flinging the bar with its orange-and-white tubes back down the incline.

After completing a full circle, Clark twirls the wheel back, arresting the spin, floors the accelerator once more, and peels away, leaving behind a cloud of blue smoke and burnt rubber on the pavement.

The car that was chasing him, having turned sharply in order to avoid the tumbling bar and lanky weighted tubes, runs off the road and disappears over the embankment.

The Escape

Earl never turned off his dazzling lights, and he presses the siren button several times to ramp it up to the loudest and wildest setting. Traffic gives way as he charges into the freeway stream and speeds ahead, changing lanes frequently to zip past unresponsive vehicles.

With the pedal still pressed nearly to the floor, Earl passes moving traffic as if it were standing still. He zooms by a highway patrol car, which seemingly ignores him—but only briefly. The officer inside, who apparently failed to heed an announcement about the chase, quickly becomes informed of the maniac in the stolen patrol car heading east. She turns everything on and speeds after him, but Earl continues to draw ahead of her with his maniacal driving.

Three lanes of the highway peel off to the south, and the former freeway becomes a two-lane highway. Ahead of him is a long backup of cars and trucks nearly at a standstill. Slowing a little, Earl takes to the oncoming lane with screaming siren and alarming lights warding off the approaching traffic.

By weaving in and out of the left lane he is able to flash by all the traffic on the right, slowing only for curves and narrowly missing oncoming vehicles.

The miles slip by quickly, and gradually the traffic thins. He is into the farming country of the Sorek Valley where he has in mind to leave the highway and follow a route on which there will be little chance of meeting another roadblock. Turning left onto an unmarked dirt road, he douses the siren and lights and speeds over the uneven terrain as fast as possible, just short of losing control of the vehicle, and soon disappears behind a hill and vanishes from view of the highway.

After some miles, the rural road makes a ninety-degree turn, taking him eastward once more.

The intense effort of the past half hour kept him from thinking much beyond each moment. Now, on this isolated stretch of the farm road, there is time to take stock of the situation he is in and consider the prospects ahead.

The Day and the Hour: Finally

What bothered him earlier returns to mind as a strong sense of destiny stemming from the realization last night that Leila has a right to know the place she has always held in his heart. There was no valid reason for him denying it; the reason had nothing to do with her and everything to do with the painful experience of his former wife having left him to marry her church's minister. There were other complications too, but he now disdains them all and counts them as nothing.

Earl fell in love with Leila over a year ago when she was presenting a paper at a security conference in Boise. He told himself it was only her professional competence that he admired. Had he admitted that she held a much wider attraction for him, it would have made no difference, for he would not have followed her to Washington DC, and any plan aimed at bringing her to him would have been a long shot indeed.

He did not speak to her at that time, but he did speak to Kevin Martin, who worked at the hotel where the event was held. Kevin then recommended the Lolomi Lodge to her. Leila liked the idea, and it put her in a mood to explore the area, which she did, and within a week she had grown to love the mountain valley.

After the conference, Earl went home and uncovered corruption involving both the former mayor and the former FSA chief. They were both removed from office, and Leila came to fill the vacancy at the FSA, stepping down from her CEO position at the national level.

It was not a scheme Earl thought would succeed. It was only a series of steps with their own benefits. He saw Leila as one who was trapped in a maze of bureaucratic pettiness that took itself to be the real world. He thought she deserved a little fresh air, which a side trip to the lodge would provide in some small measure. He knew Kevin Martin, Ken Martin's son, and was confident that their little conspiracy would work. But he saw her stepping down from her high position and coming west only in a pipe dream.

After Leila Labaki joined the Fitness Center in order to meet him—his long shot having hit its mark—he raised his guard. *He* was the mark, and he had never considered what it would mean to have her within reach; hence he forbade himself to acknowledge that his ideal had arrived. He treated it as a mystery and stashed it away in his library of riddles.

The riddle finally demanded his answer last night as he lay on Carmen's couch. With a nudge from Evelyn, his secret came out. Yes, Leila was the pearl of great price. He had found the pearl and had brought it home without possessing it. Yes, there was the irony of her becoming his formal opponent by her administrative responsibilities, but he cares nothing for that now.

Is it too late? Might there be time to show her he does not hold it against her for tethering him to her surveillance team?

It occurs to him that this extended escapade with its batch of new crimes might keep him closer to her if she can convince the FBI to let him serve a jail term at home before being taken away. But even in the worst case—if it turns out that they are separated by the Rapture—there will be a time for them.

How does he know that? This is the enigma of Earl Clark.

The country road makes a sharp left turn, now heading north. It will take him behind the Sorek Valley airstrip, on its west side. He knows exactly where the road comes out: at Highway 321 almost opposite of where Deer Drive comes down and meets the highway.

If they're waiting for me, chances are they'll have cars at Hill Street, Crossroads, and Market Street, but not here.

Earl has forgotten that, unlike his T-bird, this stolen vehicle is equipped with devices allowing it to be tracked anywhere, even when off the road. He is soon to be reminded of that fact.

As the primitive road turns to the east to skirt the airport, he is greeted by a dazzling array of lights on two patrol cars parked a quarter of a mile ahead at the highway juncture.

The only thing to do now is go back. Earl backs the car around the corner, hoping they did not see him. But the startling sounds of the latest siren hit tunes tell him that they did see him and that he has little time in which to react. The beacon tower is located at this corner of the airport. Being familiar with the service road leading to it, a narrow gravel driveway overgrown with weeds, he pulls into it far enough to be out of sight behind bushes.

The siren-and-light show comes jostling around the corner without them noticing exactly where he turned off. He gives them five seconds and then backs out and proceeds to the end of the road where it meets the highway. After the short jog on highway 321, he heads up the hill on Deer Drive.

Earl knows that the police are at that moment looking for a place to turn around—if they have not done so already—and are watching his movements on their map displays.

I've got to ditch this car.

Having sped up Deer Drive without incident, he takes the corner to Creek Street without stopping. As he flies by Grace Bible Church, he glances toward it. Several cars are there, and people are out front on the sidewalk.

Even though he concluded that the Rapture turned out to be nothing more than a small earthquake, this confirming evidence dispels lingering doubts, and he is more hopeful than ever of finding Leila waiting for him at her apartment. She would have been there at eight o'clock, he is sure of that, and there is no reason why she would have gone anywhere else on a Sunday morning.

At the foot of Creek Street he turns into the Lakeview parking lot and swings into the only vacant parking spot. He expects that they will waste some time searching for him in the restaurant.

A trail from here at the end of Lake Way leads down to the small beach park near the mouth of Gold Creek. He walks briskly to the trailhead so as not to attract attention; then, when the trail is secluded somewhat by the foliage, he breaks into a run.

At the junction with the Gold Creek trail, Earl turns left. This trail parallels the creek and will take him to a point near the end of Deer Drive where Leila's apartment building is located.

All he has to do now is watch for the bench that has S+D carved into its back. The branch trail leading up to the end of Deer Drive comes a short distance after that.

Receiving the goal of your faith, the salvation of souls.
I Peter 1:9

Chapter Three

The Moment of Truth

*A*dam and Alice Murphy arrived at the Beach House baptistery a little early. (We can call it that because nothing had happened there since yesterday's baptismal event.)

As it turned out, they had no need of an alarm clock. Alice woke up at six and found it impossible to be still and wait. After prayers and dressing, she needed to be doing something—anything—to spend nervous energy. She grabbed every clean bath towel in the house, dumped them into the back of her car, dashed back into the house, grabbed her husband—who seemed to be in a daze—and drove him to the Beach House. It was a little after seven when they arrived.

No response came to Adam's knocking on Earl's back door. The pastor was concerned about the awkward timing. He would not be comfortable doing the baptizing without Earl's permission to use the beach, let alone the house and its bathrooms. Although Earl had never turned down his requests in the past, Adam wanted to give him the opportunity. Considering the inevitability of what he was about to do—he was there by angelic authority, no less!—getting Earl's permission would seem unnecessary. To Adam it was well worth the risk: he would not ask again, but he desperately hoped Earl would say, "Yes, and may I be included?"

Murphy tried the door. It was unlocked. Footprints on the floor leading to the bathroom appeared to be from yesterday. He tried calling Earl's phone. It was unavailable. He knew what that meant. It meant that Clark was on a sensitive mission.

Adam and Alice walked over to the water's edge and stood by the dock. They intended to wait there for whomever Felix had persuaded to make this last-minute confession of faith.

The Day and the Hour: Finally

The sky was clear in the early light. Beyond the mountains in the east, a halo of pale yellow revealed the place where the sun's first rays would break over those silhouetted peaks.

Not a ripple was on the surface of the water.

The world was silent.

A poet might say nature was holding her breath.

A falling maple leaf made an audible landing.

The only sound was that of their own breathing. Thin puffs of vapor in the cool air ascended from their nostrils.

"How many did they say were coming?" Alice asked for something to say.

"Forty-nine, wasn't it?"

Alice shivered. "Our towels won't go very far," she said. "But some will benefit from having an extra one in this chilly air even if the wait is only a few minutes. I brought what we had in the house. I'll go up to the car and get them."

Adam wanted to tell her they should wait for Earl's permission, but he let her go.

As Alice walked back up the hill, putting a distance between herself and her husband, the fact of the fateful moment being only minutes away suddenly swelled to awful proportions, becoming a frightful monstrosity: the sky was about to split, and an unseen force would snatch her away. It was a violation of her being. The earth may as well open and swallow her; it came to the same thing. Every tangible element of her life that she had known and loved and trusted herself to was to be forcefully taken from her.

Opening the car door, she retrieved the towels from the cargo area and stacked them neatly on the seat.

She loved what her Maker had made and the place where he had placed her. Now this was the end of it all. It was profoundly sad and disturbing.

She lifted the stack of towels and pushed the door shut with her foot.

Alice knew something was wrong. She knew she should be glad to be going to her heavenly home, to be seeing her Maker face to face. But this was a difficult way to go. People had always said it would be a blessed privilege to bypass death in this manner. She had said so herself—it was tricky descending the steps from the driveway because she could not see ahead over the towels—but it had turned out to be a trial. Abandoning her familiar home was a sacrifice of everything—a death, really. Yes, a death is what it was.

Having reached the walkway, she managed to stay on it by looking down to the side, following the edge of the bricks.

It was easier to think of it as death. She knew that believers died every day rather than give up their trust in the goodness of God, and she had considered what she would do if that test should ever come to her. She had decided that she would die, or try to die, with praise on her lips. Now the time had come. It was time to die for him who had died for her. He had suffered unimaginable pain. For her it would be painless, as far as anyone knew—she heard Adam's footsteps coming to meet her—and she kept that thought firmly in mind and was glad.

. . .

Their plan was to commence the sacred ceremony just before the appointed hour, thus avoiding the need to change out of wet clothes. The pastor had not gotten far enough in his thinking about it to consider that it might be disrespectful to arrive in heaven dripping wet, but that thought crossed his mind at this moment, and he chuckled at the foolishness of it. But then it led to a doubt, and the doubt incited him to debate against himself:

This is like trying to force our way into heaven. Would it not be more fitting if we were dressed in our best clothes, waiting quietly in prayer?

A case could be made for that, but the traditional demonstration of faith by submitting to baptism is important.

Of course it was too late to make any other arrangement, and that reminded him that much had been left undone, and then the lateness of the hour began to torment him.

It's almost too late for anything.

The Day and the Hour: Finally

Except it was not too late for another heavy feeling of responsibility to descend upon Adam Murphy. Nearly a week ago he had come here and discussed the Rapture's timing with Earl. That meeting had taken place in Earl's shop not fifty feet from where he stood. That and the fantastic week that followed seemed to have made no difference in his friend's thinking: Earl had maintained his determination not to escape the coming troubles. Had he sufficiently impressed on his friend what that meant?

Technically, it was not too late, but very soon it would be—unless....

The doubt was there again. Nothing could be more normal than this peaceful morning. To a man who knew not the day and the hour, there would be no reason to suspect that today would be radically different from the countless mornings preceding it. There was no apparent necessity for this to be *the day*—other than the dream. Although it had occurred merely a week ago, the dream seemed distant now. The impression it made had worn thin, and its hold on his mind had softened.

Every other prophecy known to him had multiple interpretations, so why not this one? Earl's stand was not without precedent in that regard. If his disregard turned out to be appropriate, Adam would be glad for Earl. But what about the church?

Many, many others over the years had been deceived by mistaken hopes and had waited like this with bold expectation only to have their sincere faith shattered.

The day they awaited always passed the same as every day since the world began.

And with what result? he asked himself.

They got marginalized and sometimes branded heretical.

The doubt would upset his plans if given a chance to take root. It was tempting, but Adam rejected it.

It had to come sometime, and this is it. Earl has chosen to stay behind and suffer.

Still, Earl could change his mind. What if he appears in the nick of time to forbid the use of the beach?

The Moment of Truth

It wouldn't be unreasonable if he turned us out after what happened here yesterday.

Alice was coming down the hill with a tall armload of towels. She could not see over it, yet somehow she was negotiating the walkway. Adam shook off his brooding and went to help her, lifting several of them off the top of the stack which allowed her to see over the rest.

The lights and the warning whine of a newer electric vehicle announced the first arrival of Felix's converts.

This would be the first time in Murphy's career that he would baptize without having spoken at some length with each candidate. People had so many mistaken ideas about what it meant. Most had to be talked out of the idea that it secured them some privilege. A few had to be coaxed and coached into accepting what they perceived to be humiliation. It should be humbling, he would tell them. If humiliating, it was as death is humiliating, for it was a symbol of death to the proud, self-serving old nature. Even more, though, it declared resurrection to the ultimate gift of glory. All this had been symbol, hope, and expectation, not an immediate experience. Today it would be virtually immediate.

I will have little time to explain things, but some of it doesn't apply now, anyway.

It was a good thing, a beautiful thing, that these new believers wanted to be baptized. But what had Felix told them? Were they true believers or superficially swayed by one man's enthusiasm?

What a disappointment it will be if someone is left standing here alone. Or just as likely it would be a relief!

The balance of these thoughts was not helping him overcome the ever-recurring temptation to hedge his hopes.

The couple from the car were making their way down the hill. They were people he did not know. They appeared to be about his own age. Meanwhile, a van had come down the driveway, and a whole family was emerging from it.

Two ... no, three ... no, four children. I should have asked how many of the forty-nine were children.

The Day and the Hour: Finally

The youngsters were full of energy, almost falling over one another coming down the steps. Alice had gone up to meet the first couple. Adam knew he should be going to meet them too, but he was holding out for a final word from Earl.

Why did I ever consent to do this for Felix? He's a crazy man. What will they say if Earl calls it off? Worse, when the hour passes and we're still here, dripping wet, how will I explain that?

The doubt was never far away, and it would keep nagging when given the slightest chance.

Adam left it to Alice to greet the arrivals. He turned his back to them and walked to the water's edge. He knelt down on the sand beside the dock, bowing his head in a distinct attitude of prayer. This would keep him safe for a few minutes, relieving him from having to face these credulous souls who were trusting him.

He remembered Moses with his staff, the man of God who put his faith on the line at the edge of the sea.

I'm not Moses. Moses was acting on a command from above. There was no one telling me to be here doing this other than those pancake eaters. And they wouldn't come right out and admit that the Rapture was for real! ... What is for real?

He took a peek at the time: twenty minutes to go.

Only twenty minutes left of being a respectable preacher.

If his faith was still intact, his enthusiasm was at its lowest ebb. The sounds told him that more people were arriving. He marveled at their casual behavior on the brink of the catastrophe about to occur. Did they have any idea what this meant? Seen from this perspective, he could easily forget his reputation and believe it was a mistake. He yearned for a return to normal. If the prospect of departing his earthly homeland had made him more fond of it yesterday, the sensation was tenfold worse today. He had an impulse to grab the dock and hang on to dear earth.

"How ridiculous," he muttered in reaction to it.

He could hear his own answer in a voice that sounded confident and sane: "Why so, Adam? Is translation less ridiculous?"

The Moment of Truth

All of it is ridiculous! It's fantastic, the work of imagination without any basis in experience. It's only a hypothesis that few took seriously until those ridiculous dreams a week ago.

What were the chances of this hypothetical mass translation out of one space-time into another being real? Experience would say zero. The sand at his knees, the crystal water, the crisp autumn air—these things were real, and he loved them. The Rapture was an untested theory at best. But was it even that? It had been rejected by the vast majority of scholars and scientists and philosophers.

This is a nightmare. ... I'm about to join the ranks of the crackpots. How did I get into this?

Adam picked up a handful of sand and let it sift through his fingers. "This is real," he said quietly.

His whole professional life had dealt with the hypothetical, and now the thought occurred to him that his profession took itself far too seriously.

It's easy when nothing can be proven one way or the other. That's where I belong. I should never have stepped out of it and bought into this. I'm not constituted for it.

How could anyone be? No training, no lab experiments, no prototypes—just straight from tentative hypothesis to full-blown, life-or-death launching into the infinite. Yes, everything lined up with the Scriptures by a certain interpretation, but no miracle comparable to this had taken place since creation.

Seventeen minutes to go.

Indeed, it was outrageous; it *was* absurd; it was preposterous in the light of natural history. The entire vocabulary of the world had nothing to describe it.

How could I have dared to interpret things this way and been so sure of myself?

Behind him were more voices—happy voices, laughter, joy.

What am I among these? They have nothing to lose. They can afford to be happy. They'll have had a fun time. No risk of disgrace. They're all waiting for me as if I perform miracles.

The Day and the Hour: Finally

Where is your faith, Adam?

Fools believe this. There is no basis for it in reality.

Faith is holding tight to what you hope for, being sure of what you have never seen. God commended the men of old for it.

"My God, I know you can do all things; no purpose of yours can fail; I have uttered what I did not understand."

"Adam!" It was Alice's voice. "There are a lot of people here. You had better get started."

The pastor placed his hands on the dock and raised himself up, his legs tingling and shaky. He turned around and saw that about thirty people had gathered.

He made a show of looking at his watch.

Fifteen minutes to go—thirty seconds to baptize each one.

The crowd had fallen silent as soon as they saw him rise. He scanned the faces, looking for Earl. Earl was not among them. He must now assume that Earl would not be stopping him from going ahead. It was a relief to have that decided at least.

"Greetings, everyone, in the name of Jesus Christ our living Savior. Today you are declaring that the Lord Jesus is your own personal Savior, and you are trusting him with your life and eternal destiny. If you agree with that, say Amen."

"Amen!"

"All right, I'm going out ... out into the water ... like this."

He was wading out without removing even his shoes.

"I want you to come one by one. If you have a towel, leave it with Alice. As soon as you get up to your waist in the water, I'll put my hand on your back. Then hold your breath and close your eyes, crouch down a bit and lean back. I will lower you gently into the water. All right. We have to hurry. Who will be first? As soon as you've been baptized, go right back and get your towel from Alice, and then go stand on the dock."

The children were eager. One of the boys came splashing out, obviously enjoying getting his clothes wet.

"I baptize you, my brother in Christ, in the name of the Father, the Son, and the Holy Spirit."

60

Down he went, holding his nose. Up he came, spluttering and wiping water from his face.

"Okay, keep coming; we have very little time."

One by one they came—down into the water of death, up into new life in the Spirit.

He looked up and saw that more were coming down the walkway, but as far as he could see, Felix had not yet arrived.

"Quick, quick, we're running out of time! I baptize you in the name of the Father, the Son, and the Holy Spirit. Amen."

• • •

Felix set out jogging from his car and then broke into a run. He had parked fifty yards from the driveway, which was as close as he could get. Beach House Road was jammed with cars, making it impassable. His phone rang; it was Nai Meng in Nanchang, China. She had gotten through to him after trying repeatedly for the last hour. The phone system was overloaded. Twenty-three hours of her Sunday had passed, and it was nearing midnight.

"Where are they now?" Felix asked her, referring to the people who had witnessed the change in her and come to believe in the God who loves them and invites all weary travelers in life to join the congregation of sinners saved by the blood of his Son who gave himself so they could join his family and become a blessing to God himself.

"They are all here with me—in a conference room."

"Is it safe there?"

"It is not against any rule because we are employees with our families. It is not unusual for some of us to be here. Felix! What are you thinking? No place is safe for us! Whish! Just like that! We get abducted by Jesus to live with him forever!"

"How many?"

"Forty-eight, no forty-nine counting my daughter—I mean our daughter—yours too now, sweetheart. Oh, I miss you so much."

"Forty-nine! That's exactly how many are here with me to be baptized."

"Are they new believers?"

"All in the last two days."

"I know how you love them!"

"They're like my own children."

"Are you the one who told them about Jesus?"

"Yes, and I told them about you and how you became a new person and then how the old things passed away and everything became new and how I became a new person."

"We will have almost a hundred children in heaven!"

"But we will never be married—only to him, you know."

"Last night I dreamed about it. It will be awesome. We lose our old nature—that which makes so much trouble. I cannot wait to meet him. "

"I think about it all the time—crawling out of it like an ugly old shell. It really isn't me anymore."

"I know. It used to be me. Now it is a nuisance. It hangs around and trips me up all the time."

"You were pretty in your old shell; I can't wait to see you out of it. How will I find you?"

"Easy! Just ask him. You will meet him right away. It was in my dream. He has it worked out already."

• • •

"Quick, quick, we're running out of time!" exclaimed the pastor. "Sylvana! Bless you! I baptize you in the name of the Father, the Son, and the Holy Spirit. Amen."

"Here comes Felix!" someone shouted, and a cheer went up from the congregation.

"Eight minutes left!" someone announced.

Several were in the water at once, wading out and wading back. Pastor Murphy was baptizing one every ten seconds. The dock was already crowded with dripping, shivering, souls who had decided to go forward and not look back. They huddled together, trying to keep warm.

All the talking and laughing had ceased. Everyone was aware of the critical timing. The last ones were lined up now in an orderly queue on the beach.

The Moment of Truth

So many cars were jammed into the driveway and crowded on the narrow road above that latecomers had a long walk—like the elderly woman Felix was escorting down the walkway. "They're all here, every last one!" he shouted.

By the time Felix and his last convert reached the beach, one minute was left, and it appeared there would not be enough time to include everyone before the deadline. There is a limit to how quickly a person can be submerged and brought back up. Footing and hand placement have to be sure. Adam was baptizing as quickly as possible, having shortened the words to the bare minimum. Four at once were wading toward him.

"Sookie! Welcome to the family, my sister in Christ."

Someone on the dock had a waterproof timepiece and began a countdown:

"Ten."

"In the name of the Father ..."

"Nine!"

"Son, and the Holy ...

"Eight!" (Others had joined in.)

"Amen."

"Seven!"

...

"Six!"

"... the name of the Father ..."

"Five!"

"... the Son, and the ..."

"Four!"

"... Spirit. Amen!"

"Three!!"

...

"Two!!"

"In the name of the Father ..."

"One!!"

"... and the Holy Spirit ..."

"Zer ..."

The Day and the Hour: Finally

*A*huva was left staring at her phone, watching the seconds consume the final minute of the hour—the last minute of her life! She was terrified of being lifted into the clouds. Without Mark's confidence to lean on she was ill prepared to have this thing happen to her. She thought of holding onto something tightly or getting into her bedroom closet, but she was paralyzed, shaking with fear and unable to move a muscle. When the count went from 59 to 00 and the floor shook, she closed her eyes and screamed. Then all was silent. Nothing had happened.

Ahuva went rushing out of her bedroom to find her parents. She thought they would be in the kitchen, but they were not there. She called and got no answer. She found her father standing in the living room holding onto the back of a chair. He turned to face her as she came in. His face was white. There was a strange smell.

"Where's mother?"

"She vanished," he said in a voice scarcely audible.

"Where is she?"

"The Rapture."

"No, no. It didn't happen!"

"It did happen. Your mother was taken."

"No! She can't be taken. She isn't a Christian!"

"Now we find out. I've found out everything I believed all my life is wrong."

"She can't be gone, Father! The Rapture is for Christians, and I know it didn't happen yet!"

"Ahuva. ... I saw her disappear. ... Unless we're dreaming, I saw her disappear."

Ahuva stood and stared at him a moment. "I hate them!" she blurted out. "I hope Mark is gone because I never want to see him again! Boohoohoo hoohoohoo...."

Ahuva's father was not crying. He had sat down with his face in his hands. He looked up. "This is the most significant event the world has ever seen," he said calmly. "Now we know. Every question has been answered. I must find a New Testament."

> Unless you see signs and wonders, you will never believe.
> John 4:48

Chapter Four

The End of Disbelief

When Karen Martin woke this morning, the Rapture was not on her mind—in spite of the fact that she lived with a husband who mentioned it often. In fact, it never had been on her mind: all week she had busied herself seeing to the completion of the Burns house, never imagining that the Burns family might not need a house after today.

While finishing her morning's chores in the kitchen, she had heard the shouting. She had let Ken go outside, and he had gone down to the dock. Since Earl often came by in his sailboat on a Sunday morning (or if the wind happened to be calm he sometimes came down in his canoe) she had assumed that Ken was watching for Earl. She too was hoping to see Earl. She always looked forward to his Sunday visits as it was the bright spot in her week. She had not been happy to wake up to a windless morning and a glassy lake, but she hoped he would come in the canoe.

Karen had been aware of the party at the Beach House yesterday afternoon, and the sounds this morning were similar. She looked out to see Ken standing on the dock where he could see Earl's end of the bay, and evidently he saw someone there because he was grinning and waving. Perhaps Earl was coming.

She was about to go out and look for herself when the floor under her feet bounced. She lurched against the counter and steadied herself with hands against the upper cupboards. Then she turned around to look out the windows and saw strange little waves, peaks rising and falling, everywhere on the surface of the lake. Leaves were fluttering down from branches still swaying after the tremor. It had been a small earthquake. Brief quakes were not unusual, but this one had felt different.

Ken was not on the dock, and the clock was striking eight.

The Day and the Hour: Finally

Now she remembered the excitement about the Rapture prediction. This must have been it! Still, there was a possibility that Earl had come by and taken Ken in the canoe while she was engrossed in cleaning the stove.

Karen wanted to look for damage to the house, but that could wait. Dashing outside and down to the dock, she ran out to where she could see the entire bay. There was nothing in sight: no boat, no canoe. Nobody was on Earl's dock. The lake itself had become virtually calm again, little random wavelets rapidly dying.

She looked back at her house, not expecting to see any evidence of damage, and there was none. The trees were still.

It began to register in Karen Martin's mind that Ken had been taken to heaven—or somewhere—while she had been left behind. She ran back to the house, found her phone, and tried to call Earl. His phone was unavailable. She grabbed her purse, rushed out to the garage, and backed her truck out. But before she got to the Beach House driveway she saw that the road was jammed with cars. Then as she approached more closely it became evident that none of the cars were occupied and the road was impassible. (That narrow road is her only way out because it dead-ends at her house.) She attempted to call the police to report a blockage on Beach House Road, and had to leave a voice message.

But Karen had another idea. She backed up—the road being too narrow to allow her to turn around—all the way to her own driveway, parked the truck, and walked to the water's edge where the rowboat was kept resting partway out of the water. Since gasoline-powered outboard motors are no longer allowed, she had finally disposed of hers, but she could row, and it was better than sitting in the house and wondering about Earl.

Karen unsnapped its cover and shoved the rowboat out, holding the bow line and coaxing it to the dock for easier boarding. The distance by water to a place on the town waterfront where the bank is low was about two miles. First she would have to go east to clear the point of the spit, but that was much closer and quicker than it would have been to walk by way of the roads.

The End of Disbelief

A few strokes of the oars took her out beyond the end of the dock where she got a better view of Earl's place.

There is a possibility that he's there. I'd better find out.

Pointing the bow north, Karen kept a few yards from the shoreline. The surface of the water had become glassy calm. Lily-pads lined the shoreline on her right. Occasionally a ring of ripples marked the place where a fish had nipped an insect. The only sound was the creak of the rowlocks and the occasional plash of an oar when it came forward too low and scraped the surface.

Karen was not ready to entertain many implications of what had happened. Her only immediate concern was for Earl. She must find out whether he was still on earth. She desperately hoped that he was, and that she would be able to see him and talk to him. Years ago, when Martin Construction was building the Fitness Center, she had had a crush on Earl. She had kept it a secret, but now it need not be a secret, perhaps. She would tell him if she could find him.

Looking over her right shoulder she saw that Earl's float at the end of his dock was dead ahead, less than fifty yards away. The little sailboats—Walter, Willow, and Wind Chaser—lay tied to the float. Winner had been hauled out and was in the shop. She shipped the starboard oar and let the rowboat glide and drift up against the dock. As she came alongside she noticed that the planks were wet with footprints that seemed muddy.

The Beach House appeared to be deserted. It was uncanny—with all those vehicles in the driveway. She went to the back door, knocked loudly, waited, and got no answer. She tried the latch and found the door unlocked. Inside there were footprints, but no fresh, wet ones. Apparently nobody had come in this morning. She called Earl's name and got no response.

Karen checked all the rooms on the first floor and then went upstairs. The door to the room Earl used for his office stood open. She noticed a letter on his desk, written in a neat calligraphic hand and signed *Your Leila*. It was not something she wanted Earl to read. She picked it up, folded it, and put it in her pocket.

The Day and the Hour: Finally

Karen found no clue that would indicate when or why he left. He did not believe in the Rapture, and she did not believe in the Rapture. Therefore she just had to find him. Then it occurred to her that it must have been a baptizing party. She knew that Pastor Murphy sometimes used Earl's beach.

Of course. Why didn't I think of it earlier? They had one this morning, so he left—probably went to his office at the paper.

Having solved the riddle of Earl's disappearance to the best of her ability, Karen directed her thought to the next task, visualizing herself rowing to the point at the end of the spit, turning toward the town, rowing that long stretch, coming ashore at the park, and walking the half block to the paper building. Hopefully she would spot Earl's car there even before she came ashore.

What if he changed his mind about the Rapture, though. What if he's gone? Anything is possible.

Karen ran up to the garages and peeked through a window. The T-bird was gone.

"Thank God."

She hurried back down the steps and down the brick walkway. A twinge of conscience, perhaps, or something about the scene ahead made her stop in her tracks.

They were baptizing here. I've been baptized. What made them different? Ken was one of them. ... But he didn't seem different.

She resumed her walk down toward the dock but not quickly.

He tried to tell me about the Lord—as if I didn't already know. I thought he got that from his missionary grandparents. But they spent their lives in China, and he hardly knew them. He and Luke loved to talk about it. It was like a hobby, I thought. Obviously I was wrong.

Stepping up onto the dock she carefully inspected the wet footprints and wondered where the mud had come from.

They just disappeared. ... And there was that strange earthquake at the same time.

"God! I hope Earl is still here."

The End of Disbelief

Rong Li, helicopter pilot for the Shanghai Municipal Public Security Bureau, was cruising at 300 meters above the city and approaching the Shanghai Stadium. It was midnight.[1]

The white floodlights that illuminated the interior of the giant arena, five kilometers ahead, dominated the other lights of the vast city. He had been watching the space above the top of the arena intently, and there was no change in its appearance at 16:00 UTC—that is 00:00, or midnight, local time.

Five minutes before this he had made a pass directly over the stadium and had observed the seats fully occupied. The playing field was full as well, covered with thousands of invalids, most of them reclining. He had continued on, going some distance away from the arena, and then at 15:57 he had turned and aimed his aircraft directly for the stadium, keeping his eyes on it steadily.

At 16:00 he had heard a loud *pop* on the radio, and noticed a cloud forming over the arena. The lights remained steady without a flicker or momentary dimming that would have occurred if objects had risen up out of it. There had been a brief increase in the illumination, which he put down as an illusion caused by whatever atmospheric difference had formed the cloud.

Now at 16:03 he approached near enough to see down into the interior of the building. The cloud had dissipated, and he was sure there would be no difference from what he had seen on his previous pass, for he had seen nothing leave—no stream of bodies being lifted to heaven as some believed would happen.

Of course Rong Li expected nothing: if he were not sure there would be no Rapture, he would not be flying at this hour for fear of someone ascending directly under his air-machine and knocking them both out of the sky.

What he was seeing was an empty arena. The field was empty and all the seats were empty. This is exactly what the authorities—who were half insane in his opinion—wanted to happen, but it was entirely too bizarre for this airman's sensibilities.

---

1. The information behind this sketch is from a pilot's blog site I happened across.

The Day and the Hour: Finally

Rong Li had expected to be reporting that the mass of undesirable humanity which had been stuffed into the arena three days ago was still present and accounted for. He had thought this through and anticipated that the disciplinary action against the authorities who had devised this plan would be offset by the relief that no miracle had occurred. Yet it would be a horrendous job to get them out again, and he had congratulated himself on being a pilot exempt from street duty.

He switched the communication radio to Security frequency.

"Shanghai Security: Chopper seven-seven-sierra."

"*Security.*"

"Seven-seven-sierra. ... They're gone."

"*Chopper seven-seven-sierra, are you positive?*"

"Seven-seven-sierra. I'm over the stadium, descending to have a closer look. So far I see no people. The field is littered with what look like scraps of paper. There are no bodies on the field, and I see none in the seats."

"*Chopper seven-seven-sierra, land on the field if able. I'm standing by for a full report.*"

"Will comply. Seven-seven-sierra."

Descending into the brightly lit interior, Rong Li slewed his heading a full 360 degrees to view all the seats. The arena was entirely empty.

The helicopter's downdraft raised what appeared to be a cloud of smoke mixed with paper cups as it descended to the field and touched down. He shut off the engine then stepped down on dusty artificial turf under the free-wheeling rotor.

Odors of bodies, fish, and urine assailed his nostrils along with a smell he was unable to identify. Other than the paper cups and the occasional plastic bowl, there was no visible evidence of human occupation. He was stunned and stood there a long time.

Finally the rotor came to a halt, leaving it quiet enough to hear the buzzing of the stadium's floodlights.

Suddenly, from loudspeakers all over the arena, the recorded voice of Chengbo Wang boomed forth:

Everyone whom the Father gives to me will come to me.
And whoever comes to me I will never reject.
This is the reason that I came down from heaven,
not to do my own will but the will of him who sent me.
And this is the will of him who sent me:
That I should lose none of those that he has given me,
but raise them up on the last day.
Again, this is the will of my Father:
that all who look on me, the Son of God,
and believe in me shall have eternal life,
and I shall raise them up on the last day.

The voice stopped as suddenly as it had begun.

Rong Li looked up and located the windows of the control room. The building engineer was waving. He returned the gesture, climbed back into the flying machine, and filed his report with Security headquarters over the radio. Then he flipped on the electrical master, looked around perfunctorily, shouted, "Clear!" and pressed the starter.

The turbine had barely begun to spool up when it died again. Rong Li had killed it because he had seen something moving. It was coming toward him on the field. Soon he could see it was someone in a motorized wheelchair.

He waited.

As the cripple's conveyance crawled toward him, he stepped down and walked toward it, thinking this was very fortunate: he would get an eyewitness account.

A man with no legs was driving the chair. He looked pleased, as though he had something wonderful to share with the world.

"Good morning," shouted Rong Li when the eyewitness got near. "What happened to everybody?"

"They went into another universe," came the reply as the wheelchair pivoted around 360 degrees, and the unfortunate man pointed with an outstretched hand at the expanse of empty seats. "This confirms my theory! Another universe is close to ours. Very close, like almost touching. And sometimes the two universes rub together or even collide. If that happens and you happen to be at the point of collision, then you can get sucked into the other universe. I thought I was the only person that escaped until I saw you come dropping out of the black sky. Even then I wasn't sure of where I was until I saw **Shanghai Security 775** on your helicopter. Then I knew they all got swept away in a cosmic tsunami, and only I was fortunate enough to be left behind. Too bad for them!"

"How do you know the other universe isn't better than this one?"

"It could be. But we know that nearly all of this universe is uninhabitable. Same with the others, is what I think."

"What did you actually see?"

"They just vanished."

"Is that all? Where did the fine dust come from?"

"There was a jolt, like an earthquake, when they got enveloped in smoke or fog. The dust—I do not know."

"Instantly? One moment they were all here, and the next moment they were gone?"

"They stood up first, then they melted away in the cloud."

"You don't mean they *all* stood up, do you?"

"The ones I could see did. That's the part that surprised me."

"Were you down here on the field when it happened?"

"Oh yes. Wheels and stairs do not mix, you know."

"I flew over while this place was full. It looked like most of them out here on the field were lying down, not sitting or standing. I figured they were the weakest ones. Now you're telling me they stood up?"

"Unless my eyes deceived me, which is possible."

"Did someone come along and help them up?"

"No. They just got up."

"Just like that, huh? Were they saying why they were getting up?"

"No. Nobody said anything."

"Had they been talking up to that point?"

"It was terrible. If you saw how they were packed in here you would not ask that."

"Are you telling me it suddenly went silent?"

"Yeah. I told them to shut up."

"And they all heard you and quit talking. Is that what you want me to believe?"

"Not right away. But it came right after that."

"What came right after that?"

"Well, they lit up."

"What do you mean, 'They lit up?'"

"It was like they became white lights—bluish white."

"Was that before or after they stood up?"

"It was before. That's when they quit talking."

"So they became white lights. Were they faint, like ghosts?"

"Not at first, but they faded away in a fog like ghosts."

"Now let me get this straight. They looked like bluish white lights. Do you mean their faces turned white?"

"No. Everything."

"Clothes and all?"

"Clothes and all. It was like everything that was in contact with them glowed."

"It sounds like some kind of aura, an electrical phenomenon. Were they all just standing there when they faded away?"

"They were looking up, like they saw something in the air, and they raised their hands."

"And you. ... Did not the blue-white glow come upon you too?"

"I did not think so at the time."

"What made you different? Were they doing anything different from what you were doing?"

"Before it started, you mean?"

"Yes, before it started."

"They were all talking about the Christ religion. I could not stand it."

"So you told them to shut up?"

"I did. I told them to shut up and go to hell."

The Day and the Hour: Finally

Through his stateroom window, Ernie was intent on watching the rocky shorelines of evergreen-forested islets slip by, for they were surprisingly close. He was dressed and ready for breakfast. It seemed unlikely that the day would be interrupted by an act of God. He believed it was a possibility, and he might even say it was quite probable if you had asked him, but there was nothing he could do about it, so he let the scenery be the extent of his world and focused his thoughts on rocks and trees while he waited for Enid. Should the hour come and nothing happen, at least he was ready for breakfast.

Enid was in the head—or the bathroom as she called it—finishing her dressing and what Ernie called her decorating for whatever she was dressing and decorating for. We might assume it was for her heavenly debut, but thinking about being whisked away at any moment was far too scary. It had been a fun cruise up to this point; her dream had been fulfilled, and she would ask nothing more. She was letting hair and makeup be everything: there were certain steps that had to be taken, and she was going to execute them to the best of her ability. She was not watching the time; she had no idea what she would do if she finished before eight o'clock.

• • •

On the bridge of the cruise ship the first mate was hand-steering the vessel through the narrows on her way south. Normally the autopilot did the steering: the navigational system knew the exact location relative to the planned route, and it kept the vessel precisely on the line at all times. But in a tight spot like this the autopilot was not used. Steering was done by hand in narrow places because there would be no time to make corrections if the automatic system failed.

The channel looked uncomfortably narrow for the size of his ship, but the helmsman knew it was only an illusion. He had been through here many times. Today he had come close to telling the captain on duty that he was not feeling well and needed to be relieved. But it would have been a lie. He was not ill: the Rapture was on his mind. He was a new believer—since last night only. He had taken in the Jayson North show and been convicted by some-thing the comedian had said: "Once you're in hell, you're stuck there forever, so if you ignore what I'm telling you now, *make sure you want to go to hell and stay there!*" It struck him that hell was a real place. He had never before taken that word to be any-thing but a symbol for extreme discomfort. As hard as he tried, he could not undo what had been done by those words and go back to letting it be merely a swear word. So he went forward. "If you're not saved already, claim the blood of Jesus Christ to cover your sins," Jayson had said. So he did, and immediately he felt better. "Forget the Rapture," Jayson had added (for he wanted everyone to understand that in the overall scheme of things whether the Rapture occurred or not was not the important thing).

Why isn't it a big deal? The helmsman wondered. Why would it not be a big deal to find yourself suddenly transported to another dimension—or wherever it was that heaven was located. But he had to leave off wondering and pay close attention because a sharp turn to port was coming up. The tide level was high and the current was running with the ship, which meant he needed to execute a tighter turn, and it was time to initiate the maneuver.

• • •

The captain, in his staterooms located just aft of the bridge, was watching news reports:

It was revealed this morning that a summit conference of religious leaders was called last week, the first of its kind to meet in the Pyramid of the Nimrod Tower in the Great City. Simultaneously, the pope made an announcement: all Mideast nations have signed on to a ceasefire, pending a new ordering of world powers that will be taking place after the Removal.

This just in: An Iranian cruise missile with a nuclear war-head, flying low, was downed between Jerusalem and Tel Aviv. The warhead failed to detonate. This is the war that Israel has been warning the world of. If Israel follows through, we can expect an all-out war between the two nations.

The Day and the Hour: Finally

The unquenchable conflict between those two countries was nothing new. What got the captain's interest was the mention of the "Removal," which he understood to be an alternate term for the more common "Rapture" used by those who welcomed it the most. He had been trying to make sense of the Rapture controversy and why it had become so important that a summit conference was needed. Never had the preposterous notion of masses of people instantly disappearing from earth been anything but the script of a comedy carried out by crazed cultists and media opportunists. Was there something more behind it? Had the intelligence hidden in the space signals been recovered? Did world leaders know about an alien takeover? Was there some advanced technology from elsewhere in the universe about to be applied to vaporize those who would oppose a new world order?

In addition to the news desk, the captain had three channels up on the screen displaying views of the interiors of mega churches, all showing the countdown. 3 ... 2 ... 1 ... 0. The moment of truth had arrived!

But nothing happened, just as he had expected.

The captain stood up, stretched, and yawned, then decided he would go for breakfast. He opened the door to the bridge, and seeing ahead through the wheelhouse windows it was obvious to him that the ship needed to be turning; but the ship definitely was not turning, and no one was on the bridge. The helmsman had left his station, and the ship was failing to make a critical turn. In fact, she was heading directly for a reef which he knew extended out a long way from the rocky shore, hidden below the surface.

He rushed to a steering station and threw the lever hard to port, but it was too late, for the momentum of a massive vessel must be managed in a timely manner. The ship began a slow roll to starboard, but no quick response in the direction of travel would result. In a matter of seconds the bow would be contacting the reef. He threw the propellers into reverse, but the response from that would not be soon enough to arrest the ponderous forward momentum.

The End of Disbelief

* * *

From what Ernie could see through his cabin window, he thought the rocks were coming awfully close, but he had heard others tell of going through the narrows, and he knew what to expect.

For all his attempted nonchalance, Ernie had been nervously watching the time, and when the minute went from 59 to 00 he had closed his eyes and held his breath.

When nothing happened, he stood up and shouted: "I've won my bet!"

Enid popped out of the bathroom. "You mean there's no Rapture, and I've gotten dressed up for nothing?" Her attempt to make light of the nonevent was not convincing. She was relieved, but she was distressed too. She was glad to be in the security of the ship and not out in space somewhere, but something was not right about everything that had once mattered and was supposed to have mattered more.

"Come on, let's go to breakfast. I'm hungry," said Ernie.

As he spoke, he felt the ship begin to roll to starboard, indicating that it was negotiating a sharp turn to the opposite side. Ernie was anxious for a better view, and he prompted Enid to get her purse and anything else she needed and to hurry.

As she stepped back into the head for a moment, a shudder and a shaking shot though the ship; their stateroom bounced and tilted, and a sickening screech of steel plate being tortured and torn was very close, for their stateroom was well forward on one of the lower passenger decks.

Enid screamed and lost her footing and fell. Ernie braced himself. The room began tilting the other way now as the ship slowly rolled toward the port side.

Sirens sounded in the passageway outside their door.

After striking the reef, the momentum of the massive vessel drove her forward and forced the crumpled keel up onto the rock, lifting her bow and causing her to lose some of her stability. She began leaning alarmingly to the port side.

The Day and the Hour: Finally

Naturally it was a bad scene in the dining rooms above: everything on the tables—dishes and food, glasses and drink—went sliding off, crashed to the floor, and scooted across the deck.

It was scary in some of the port-side cabins too: the lowest ones aft near the stern had seawater rising above their portholes.

Being on the starboard side in an outboard cabin such as the one Ernie and Enid occupied, it was downward to the stateroom door. But opening the door against gravity and making room for it to swing back was a feat that took all of Ernie's strength and agility.

In the intervals between sirens, announcements were being made in several languages. They had not yet heard the English version; it had been Spanish, and presently it switched to some oriental language which Ernie guessed was Hindi. But he needed no announcement to know what to do. Common sense told him to make his way to the lifeboat deck on the lower side of the ship—the side opposite of where they were located at present.

Outside their stateroom door the corridor was chaotic. The ship was now heeled to such an angle that one had to brace oneself against the bulkhead on the lower side of the hallway. Some people were crawling on hands and knees, and it was difficult to get around them. Doorways stood open on the lower side, and each one presented a challenge because it was difficult to pass by without falling into the open cabin. Some of the doors on the uphill side, the ones to the outboard cabins like the one Ernie and Enid had successfully exited, had not yet been gotten open to free the occupants. Ernie tried to help get one of them open by pushing on it, but the angle of the deck was too steep to get a good footing, and the corridor was too wide to reach across.

Sounds were deafening. Between alarms and the blaring instructions—now in Chinese—people were shouting to one another and complaining about the lack of help from the crew. Some were wailing loudly. Children were crying.

Enid realized she was not going to have a good day. She bravely tried at first to keep up with Ernie. He would get around the crawlers by putting both his hands on the wall and side-stepping past them. Enid tried to follow his example, but she soon encountered a knot of bodies that she couldn't bridge: she was not tall enough to reach the wall with her hands while stepping by the obstacle with her feet. Someone was pushing her from behind and she nearly collapsed onto the immobile bodies.

Ernie kept looking back to make sure his wife was coming. When he realized that she was stuck, he wanted to go back to help her, but there was no returning against the flow; he had to keep moving. Everyone was trying to move toward the stairway going up to the next deck level.

Seeing that he was continuing on without her, Enid became desperate. It would be hopeless trying to catch up to him by crawling on hands and knees, which appeared to be the only option left to her. She sat down on the spot, her back against the lower wall, pulling her legs up tight to let others crawl by; she bowed her head and wept quietly. Everything had gone wrong. The wonderful cruise had become a nightmare. The Rapture had failed. Was there no God? Her heart cried out to him just in case he was there—in case he cared to listen to her. It was a cry without words, not a plea for help, and not a prayer for rescue. It was a plea for the comfort of a father, for arms to embrace her. She pictured a hiding place under the wing of a mother bird, enfolding her in soft down. She clung to the image. Whatever happened, she would stay where she was. If the ship sank she would trust the feathers of her nestling place to keep her dry.

There was no danger of the ship sinking immediately because rocks gripped her crumpled forefoot. But flooding was taking place through openings in the depressed stern on the port side, and this was gradually reducing stability and increasing the angle of list.

Having lost sight of Enid, Ernie tried reaching her by phone, but she did not answer. He thought most likely she had left her phone in the stateroom. He could only hope she was making progress in the same direction he was going.

The Day and the Hour: Finally

The stream of bodies in which Ernie was moving had brought him to the first stairway. He knew there would be four more of these before he would reach lifeboat level where he could cross over to the port side. Negotiating the stairs was somewhat less difficult than the corridor had been since there were no doorways.

Before Ernie got to the top of the stairway, the press came to a standstill, and angry voices began to dominate the constant background of grunts and sobs and cursing and wailing. He could move neither forward nor backward because people were closely pressed against him on every side. Someone had vomited on the spot where he was standing, and that together with other smells made it hard for him to breathe.

Eventually the crowd began to move again, but very slowly, and when he got to the landing at the next deck level the reason for the slowdown became apparent: everyone from that deck—or at least those who had been able to get out of their staterooms—had pressed into the stairway up to the next level ahead of those coming up from lower levels.

Meanwhile, the angle of list had increased to the point where it was acknowledged that deployment of the lifeboats on this side had become impossible, just as Ernie had assumed would be the case. Word of it came out on the emergency speaker system, first in English, and they were advised to continue going up, all the way up to the top deck.

Almost immediately the instruction was reversed. Because of the critical stability situation, everyone on the starboard side of the ship was ordered to descend immediately to a lower deck and wait there for further instructions. It was repeated in other languages for those who had heard but not understood, while crudely stated opinions flowed freely about chances of being saved.

The report of the grounding of the cruise ship had reached the Coast Guard, and rescue vessels of various types and sizes were on the way from a nearby city, but it would be some time before everyone would be taken off the ship, and Ernie would have to wait a long while for his breakfast.

One is taken, and one is left.
Matthew 24:40,41

Chapter Five

One Taken, One Left

*T*he priest serving the Old Catholic Synergistic Church where Harold Foster's former boss got her spiritual guidance suddenly become a fan of the Rapture on Friday. The question was settled for him after he verified information from the occult side which Neva had provided: one hundred percent of spiritualists believed in the removal of Christian saints by some means. This was enough to convince him that a significant event would occur.

That meant he had to devise an appropriate response based on a true interpretation of the event. He disagreed with the Roman Catholic interpretation; he was not so spiritually benighted as to believe it could be a "removal of the reformers" by aliens from another planet—as the Church had been advertising. Of course, neither could he go along with the idea that it was a resurrection and flight to heaven to be enjoyed by people who had no credentials other than some undocumented declaration of personal faith. Rather than accept anything that others were saying, he combined standard pretribulation Rapture doctrine with exclusive rites of his denomination and called it the "Supreme Rite of the Rapture of the Saints."

Fr. Newagger claimed to value love, joy, and peace above everything. These were his ideals, he often said, and he sought them along any avenue where similar things were on the signposts. While he made use of age-old Catholic rituals, he incorporated elements from other faiths and perspectives in his teaching.

After this resourceful clergyman had become convinced that the Rapture signified the beginning of the end of the age, implying that his teaching about the new age of peace having dawned was premature, he adopted a view of biblical prophecy that, for him, was radical. He said the Bible must be taken seriously at least concerning the calamities soon to befall the earth, and he designed a special service that would compensate for mistaken dogma and transfer his worshipers from regular ritual rolls to the blessed roster of the Rite of the Rapture which he had invented for his peculiar flock. It was to be a service of power, using the most potent rites from several traditions. During his preparations he had secured a promise from the Queen of Heaven.

Not being limited to official dogma, as many of his Roman brethren were, he did not allow himself to be fooled by the counterfeit Marian oracles that had been casting the Rapture in a negative light. No, his motive was pure. He had been heard by the Virgin, the true Queen of Heaven, and she had told him that his parishioners would get the same favor that had been bestowed on the congregations of those who had received the Rapture dream.

His plan was to offer his specially-enhanced Mass just before *the Hour* in order to maximize its effect. This would place the service a little more than three hours ahead of the Sunday schedule that people were used to. He had notified everyone who had ever attended his little church and for whom he had an email address, a list of one hundred names. He had gotten ten positive replies. But he was not discouraged, expecting that a few more would attend when they saw the day and the hour drawing near. As it turned out, the total attendance was three, Harold Foster's former boss, Neva, being among them.

The moment had come, and his timing was perfect. The Eucharist had been consummated, and he stood facing the image of the Virgin, his arms outstretched to receive her blessing on behalf of the congregation. His eyes were closed, and when the floor shook he lost his balance and nearly fell. He grasped the edge of the rickety table on which the tabernacle stood, and in doing so jerked it away from the wall, causing the tall box to rock backward, striking the wall, then fall forward on its face. Seeing what had happened, he fainted.

No one else in the room fell. Neva was enough of an engineer to know that the probability of a sharp quake of such short duration happening at exactly the predicted eight o'clock was infinitesimal—essentially impossible as a coincidence of independent natural events. An earthquake would not be an unlikely adjunct to bodily resurrections. It simply meant she had missed out.

The other two congregants rushed forward to assist Fr. Newagger. Neva was not feeling kindly toward him at that moment, and she sat down.

Neva had sought forgiveness, under Newagger's direction, after hearing Clio's testimony. She followed his recipe which called for confession and penance. Though it had been the priest's prescription that sent her to learn the ways of witches, she had formally renounced her association with them.

She had done the best she could, but it was not good enough. She wondered whether Clio had been taken, and she reached into her purse for her phone but stopped short of completing the call. She knew the answer: Clio had been transformed. She had seen it; it was unmistakable. But rather than trust a woman, she had trusted the wisdom of Fr. Newagger.

Harold knew the way and could have helped her, but he was overshadowed by the threat of his wife, and Neva would not risk losing her lead engineer over a domestic dispute. She could have quietly inquired after the faith he held and the way he walked, but she took a route in which she remained the driver that ultimately led her into desperate and despicable acts. She had thought she was doing better than associating with common, hypocrite-ridden churches; she had separated herself from them by her sincerity. It now had become clear that sincerity was her only plea, and sincerity was useless when attached to the wrong thing.

Neva stood up and left the small room that served as the meeting place of the OCSC. It had failed her twice. In the last four days she had succeeded in transferring her hopes for a bright future from her worldly career to a heavenly one. It had seemed to her a miracle that she had made such a change. Now must she go back?

The Day and the Hour: Finally

It seemed impossible to go back, but yet she would need her job in order to live. What if Harold's colleague Jim had been taken? She knew Harold had been evangelizing Jim. Without either of them on her team, the MAD project would be dead. She would have to face the consequences and hope she would not be fired.

Arriving back at her house, Neva noticed the e-book stick she had brought home from the office lying on the table. She had found it on her desk and asked Jim about it. He said Harold had given him one that looked just like it. Now she picked it up and pressed the on/off button at the end of the pen-like device. Out of it sprang a tube that unrolled to form a flat sheet, the screen of an e-book reader displaying a note page bearing two short lines:

> I am the way, the truth, and the life.
>
> No one comes to the Father but by me.
>
> – Jesus

She touched the screen and the note vanished. Showing in its place was the listing of books the device held: Genesis, Exodus, Leviticus ... Matthew, Mark, Luke, John ... Revelation.

Neva decided she would use what Harold had left her and make this her new project. Whatever would come of her job, she would do what she had to do; then she would come home each day and pursue the path that Clio had taken and offered to her. She had refused it once, and that was a huge mistake. But she remembered Clio saying she would be praying for her. Neva would rely on those prayers and Harold's gift. Now she would study the way that Scripture revealed and leave the priest to his own devices.

She sat down and touched *Genesis* on the screen.

> In the beginning, God created the heavens and the earth.

There was a reference mark on the verse, and she touched it.

> In the beginning was the Word, and the Word was with God, and the Word was God.

She touched the reference verse, and it took her to the book of John, and there she began reading.

84

One Taken, One Left

*A*fter enjoying Sunday-evening dinner at Mulla's on the Mall, Larry and Lucy Link went up to their little room in the Spartan quarter of the great hotel, arriving there about 6:30.

Though they had not mentioned it to one another since leaving home, neither of them had entirely forgotten the Rapture. It was no surprise that no one was talking about being whisked away tonight, and neither did they hear any debate on the subject. There was not even ridicule about it in the Great City as far as they could tell. Apparently no one there had heard about the dreams; otherwise the subject surely would have come up. This lack of concern made it seem, from the vantage point of this triumphantly cosmopolitan city, that the Rapture was a matter of quaint American folklore. Nevertheless, they could not help being a little apprehensive. The whirlwind tour of the Alexander Hotel today had almost, but not quite, made them forget. Larry was the more apprehensive, or so he thought, and he determined to keep Lucy in sight and preferably hold on to her physically until the eight o'clock hour had passed.

But Larry had miscalculated. At seven o'clock Lucy disappeared.

He did not witness her vanishing because she had gone into the bathroom. When a mild earthquake caused the floor to shake, he heard a thump and a clattering sound from that direction, and the bathroom door rattled. He rushed to the door and called.

"Are you alright?"

There was only silence.

Larry opened the door and saw that Lucy was not present. He saw no evidence of a mishap, but there was vapor and smoke in the air and a strange smell that reminded him of breaking rock.

Then it struck him: maybe he had the time wrong. Eight o'clock had stuck in his mind because that was the hour everyone talked about back home—eight o'clock in the morning. He knew Iraq was about halfway around the world, so twelve hours of time-zone difference seemed right.

The Day and the Hour: Finally

Lucy was not there, and he had seen no evidence that her body had been extracted. If she had been Raptured, everything she wore had gone with her, contrary to what someone had told him last week.

She must have slipped out and gone somewhere.

But where would she have gone without telling him? That would be unlike her, unless she were angry with him. But she had not been angry with him during the last few minutes—far from it. In fact, she had told him she loved him, which he had wondered about because he could see no reason for it at that time. It had not occurred to him to connect it with the Rapture.

Did she go into the bathroom just then because she knew she would be leaving at seven o'clock? If she had gone for another purpose, there was no evidence of it. He looked again to be sure and decided that the smoke must have been very fine dust, for it was settling on the floor. And her phone was on the floor too.

She must have known it was at seven but wasn't sure she'd be going.

To be saying goodbye without being sure she would be leaving would have been awkward.

Or if she knew she was going, she also knew I wasn't, and couldn't bear to tell me.

The truth was only too clear: the sounds were caused by the air closing in, filling the space where she had been.

Yes, Lucy was gone. The fine dust was all that was left of her.

Junior was still with him, lying in the middle of the floor. Larry was thankful for that.

But Lucy was definitely gone—gone on some great adventure in a different mode of existence, never to return. Most likely she would be unwilling to come back even if she could. She may have forgotten about him already, being in a whole new mode of existence with other companions. But whether she remembers him or not he will never know. Life with Lucy had ended.

Larry checked his phone to see if she had possibly left him a message. Nothing. No, and there never will be anything.

fter presenting last night's lesson to the church which met at the Lakeview restaurant, Clio had gone home exhausted. She slept well, rose early this morning, and went back to the Lakeview to help set up for breakfast and serve the congregation their last meal on earth. But instead of joining them as they ate, she took a piece of toast and a cup of coffee into Margaret's office and sat down with her book. She was finishing the chapter on Elijah, ancient Israel's most colorful and influential prophet. She had come to the end of his life.

Studying the life of Elijah, Clio had learned about the trials he had suffered while standing against devil worship and proclaiming one true God. She wrote about Northern Israel's king Ahab who for economic and political expediency had married pagan Jezebel, daughter of the king of Tyre. Jezebel sought to make Baal worship the standard religion in Ahab's court, and through her influence a center of Baal worship was established in Samaria.

This was a painful experience for Clio. She had repented of her own promoting of anti-Christian doctrine; she believed she was forgiven, but she could not help seeing herself in Jezebel. She was not concerned about losing or gaining her salvation. She trusted God; she trusted that whatever he did with her would be good. Whether he condemned her, as she deserved, or whether he decided to include her in the congregation of the redeemed through the blood of Christ—whichever way he chose for her, it would be good. She had dedicated herself to worshiping the true God as revealed in the Hebrew and Christian Scriptures, and he was good. He was her sovereign, and his judgments were perfect. "Thy kingdom come; thy will be done," had become her motto. She was Jezebel no longer; Elijah was her hero, and she fancied confronting the witches she knew and bringing down fire from heaven to devour their ridiculous sacrifices.

This turnaround was very recent for Clio, and the illumination she had gotten from studying the Bible was very new. Because of her background she did not consider herself worthy to be in full fellowship with the Lakeview church. Although she had been its first member and its teacher, she viewed herself as the servant, not the equal of those folk. They were all in attendance this morning, eagerly expecting to be included in the translation of the Rapture, and it was all very new for them too! She marveled at their single-minded faith and enthusiasm for the next stage of their lives, but she was not sure about herself. None of them had been as bad as she had been, according to her own judgment, although she understood that God was not judging her that way.

Clio had buried herself in compiling the history book from which she taught, and now she saw that it was an unworthy thing. She had felt compelled to do it out of her love of history, but she doubted whether it could truly have been the Lord's will.

Although these thoughts bubbled up from time to time, they made her more intent on doing the writing, for as long as she worked on the book she was at peace.

Clio did not own a computer or any other electronic device for writing. Her only concessions to modern technology were her electric motorcycle and the dinerPad she used when on duty in the restaurant. She wrote with pen and ink, filling up the blank pages in her large notebook.

Elijah knew he was about to be taken to heaven, but his servant Elisha was not sure he would be privileged to witness his master's translation. Would he simply disappear, or would he see him go? As the two of them talked about it, a fire in the form of chariots and horses came between them, and Elijah went up in..

Before Clio completed that last sentence, a glow illuminated the Lakeview dining room as well as Margaret's office: each person was briefly transfigured by a bluish-white light shining from within. The phenomenon lasted only a moment before fading away, and when it did no one was left anywhere in the building.[1]

---

1. Perhaps I will explain later how I know this. I assume the same thing happened to Clio because I found her book open with the pen laying on it and the last sentence unfinished. I found fine dust everywhere.

One Taken, One Left

*A*ccording to the notes he left behind, Hunter Martin had stayed up all night reading his wife's Bible.

After being baptized yesterday afternoon he went home and told Hilda he wanted to find out for himself what the Bible said about the Rapture. She told him to read the last few verses of First Thessalonians chapter four, which he did. Then he closed the Book, opened it at the beginning, turned past the first few introductory pages, and began reading chapter one of Genesis.

"You're wasting your time if you think you'll find something about the Rapture in the Old Testament," Hilda advised him.

Hunter looked at her as if he had not understood what she said.

"I said—"

"Yes, I know. I have a theory about the resurrection. There's a fundamental incompatibility between our bodies and where we're going. Heaven is a spiritual place, and bodies are physical."

"Read it again," she countered. "It says we'll be caught up in the clouds to meet the Lord in the air."

"No, it says the dead in Christ rise first, and then we who are alive will be caught up together with them to meet the Lord in the air. I'm sure you don't think bones and ashes will have flesh put on them so they look respectable when we meet in the air. Obviously that makes no sense. But clearly they get caught up slightly ahead of us. Does that mean the clouds will be full of fragments of disintegrated bodies when we get there? I hope not."

"So what are you saying, Hunter? Do you think only our spirits leave the earth?"

"No, because the text makes a point to say that the dead rise first. Aren't the spirits of dead Christians already in heaven? So it must be about their bodies and our bodies too—at minimum. Therefore, if the literal meaning is nonsensical, the language about rising to meet the Lord in the air has to mean something else. Paul—it was written by Paul, right? ... Paul got the word from the Lord and expressed it as best he could, I'm sure, but behind those words must stand something as mysterious as creation. That's why I'm reading Genesis: to see if there's a principle common to both."

"I'll save you the trouble," said Hilda. "God formed man from the dust of the earth and breathed the breath of life into his nostrils, and he became a living soul."

Hunter closed the Book and laid it down.

"So what happens if that process is reversed? First the breath of life returns to God, and then the body turns to dust."

"Then you end up with nothing," she declared.

"Did God create Adam's spirit when he breathed the breath of life into his body?" Hunter asked.

"As far as I know he did."

"I beg to differ with you. 'When' is a time word. Spirit is not physical. Only physical things exist in time because time is a property of physical mass. So in terms of our world, we have to say that spirit has no beginning or end. Therefore Adam's spirit joined his newly created body. Now when that gets reversed, the spirit of man is released from the body but is not destroyed."

"But that was Adam."

"Sure. What does the name Adam mean? I saw in a footnote where it means 'man.' We're all descendants of Adam, aren't we? Then we're all represented in Adam. So I figure that after the Rapture they're going to find little piles of dust! You see, my dear, this thing is beyond anything that has happened since creation. Creation is a miracle because it's an act that exists outside our material universe. Likewise the Rapture and Resurrection are miracles because they're not connected with any physical process. The Bible makes it sound like they are, but you quickly see that the words 'caught up,' 'clouds,' and 'air,' stand for what cannot be described in our world."

"Isn't heaven out there somewhere beyond the stars?"

"Right. And we have to pass through clouds to get there."

"You're making fun of me."

"You can think of heaven that way, if you like."

"I don't understand anything you're saying, Hunter. You say it's about our bodies, but you say our bodies are physical and can't exist in heaven, and so they turn to dust."

"I did say our bodies are physical, but they're not entirely physical. What we call physical things aren't entirely physical because they're based in information. Information is not a physical thing. There is no reason that information cannot exist in a non-physical realm like heaven. If you take all the information that organizes our bodies away, you get water and a pile of dust. But the information that once held it together may still exist in another form. So our bodies have a heavenly form based on the same general plan our earthly bodies have. The Resurrection and Rapture both make use of such information to construct new bodies while the Rapture releases the spirit from the body as well as its information. So there you have it. That's my theory."

"You won't find any of that in the Bible, I'm sure."

"Are you sure? How many hours do I have? Seventeen plus? Let me see what I can find."

Thus Hunter got himself into a Bible study that lasted all night and took almost every minute before he became dust.[1]

While browsing through the Old Testament, he got off on another subject. He became interested in the promise Yahweh God made to Abraham in Genesis 12:3:

> I will bless them that bless you, and him that curses you I will
> curse, and in you all the families of the earth will be blessed.

And later in Genesis 17:7:

> I will establish my covenant between me and you and your seed
> after you throughout their generations for an everlasting covenant
> —to be a God to you and to your seed after you.

There was nothing required of Abraham in order to maintain the blessing, so why was it announced if not to induce good behavior? Why was it even mentioned? What was it that Abraham needed to know? Hunter wondered about these things and more.

---

1. I found in his notebook the outline of this theory, and to make it presentable I cast it as a conversation with his wife.

The Day and the Hour: Finally

As the morning light brightened the sky, Hunter found an answer in Galatians 3:8. But then it dawned on him that he had forgotten his purpose and had nothing to tell his wife. He had become familiar with the concordance at the back of her Bible, and now he hastily began looking up verses where the word *dust* appeared. And presently Hilda appeared.

"Listen to this!" was Hunter's Rapture-day greeting to his wife. "Job 34:15: 'All flesh will perish together, and man will turn again into dust.' Sounds about like the Rapture, doesn't it?"

"No, the Rapture isn't about perishing. It's about going to heaven," she replied (being wide awake, for she knew the hour).

"All right. I see your point. Here's another one: Ecclesiastes 12:7: 'And the dust returns to the earth as it was, and the spirit returns to God who gave it.' There! We have Creation in reverse, don't you agree?"

"What dust is that about?"

"It's the dust our bodies are made of when you take out the all the wisdom that holds it together—wisdom as in Proverbs 8:26."

"But what you read in Ecclesiastes doesn't say anything about 'wisdom,' just 'spirit.' When people die and the spirit leaves the body, the body doesn't immediately return to dust!"

"No, of course not. But in time it does because the information has been interrupted and cannot do its job."

"So you admit that the information is still in the body when a person dies. Then does it gradually seep away? What happens in cremation? It gets destroyed immediately!"

"Well, the same information can be in more than one place at the same time. Whenever information is used, we find it being copied over and over. So why not let a copy of the information in your DNA be in heaven ready to be used in your new body?"

"Why not take it there when you fly to heaven? Why do you want to make it more complicated than it needs to be?"

"Okay, you can go your way, and you can tell me how it was passing through the clouds. They're nothing more than fog banks in the sky, you know."

One Taken, One Left

*L*aura and her two children were presumably ready and waiting at eight o'clock because when Jake checked on the house shortly after eight he found it empty.

Everything was in order. Laura had left the key to her car along with the key to the house on the kitchen table.

This was Jake's first encounter with something that confirmed disappearance, and to say it was unnerving is an understatement. At first glance there was nothing that he could not explain by Laura simply having left. The motive could have been the two months rent that was overdue. But on closer inspection he found jackets and a purse hanging on hooks by the door, and on the floor next to the table he found a phone.

Also on the table he found a note addressed to him, and beside it a two-page letter Laura had left which was intended for Veronica Sweet.[1]

Dear Jake,

I hope you do not get this but if you do I want to thank you for renting your house to me and Emma and Emmett.

You can have the car and everything in it. I put all our belongings in it. It isn't worth much. The battery is very weak. The registration is here and I signed it. You can fill in the rest. I hope it will not be very much trouble for you.

There is also a letter I wrote to Veronica Sweet. If she is still here could you see that she gets it? Or if you are not here and she is, I hope someone will find it and give it to her. If she is not here I hope someone will read it. I left it open as you can see. I hope it will encourage someone.

God bless you. You have been very kind to us.

– Laura

---

1. Jake did not know whether Veronica would still be available, so he left the letter on the table and told me about it.

Dear Veronica,

I am sorry that I had to go so soon. I hope things work out well for you and Valentine. Or if Valentine is not with you I hope you will forgive Emma for taking her with her. I hope you know what I mean. It is very difficult to say.

I do not know why it was easy for me. Mr. Clark told me about the Rapture one week ago. After that everything was different. I couldn't stop thinking about going to be with God.

I was asked how I knew it was true. I know the Bible talks about it but Mr. Clark told me something that made me very happy. He said he wouldn't be surprised if God wanted me to be with him in heaven. Then he explained who Jesus was and told me I could belong to him if I wanted to! And I did!!!

So if you read this don't look for me. I'm really not here anymore. I wish you could have believed in Jesus

and the Bible. I know you are interested in heaven. I think everyone is. Don't you? Earth is good too. I mean God created everything so everything has to be good. But lots of things don't work out very well. Do you wonder what God will do? I know he will make sure earth turns out to be good too.

I don't think you have to worry that everything will keep going wrong for ever. God wouldn't allow that, would he? I don't think so. When I thought about this I wondered why he was taking Christian people out of the world. I know some people think Christians are not helping to make the world better but I don't believe that. All of the ones I know are trying to be helpful to others. So I think we will be coming back and I will meet you again!

Yours forever,

-Laura

Samson reached out to the two central pillars on which the house rested
and leaned upon them, one with his right hand, the other with his left.
Judges 16:29

Chapter Six

Mission Accomplished

We left Earl Clark on the Gold Creek trail, fleeing his pursuers and running toward his goal, his only goal, the one thing he must do this morning. In spite of certain signs to the contrary, he has set aside the possibility that the Rapture occurred—and even if it did occur, apparently not everyone was taken, for he saw evidence of that as he passed by Grace Bible Church.

The one thing that matters to him now is convincing Leila that he loves her above all others and that she will be his perfect bride. He knows he must bear the penalty for opposing the works of the enemy, but after that has been accomplished there will be time for them. He believes that none of his crimes are serious enough to put him at risk of lengthy incarceration, a two or three year stay at most, and they both have means that can be brought to bear to ensure minimum sentencing and perhaps immediate parole.

Resistance to the Reorganization, that effort to which he was energetically dedicated before today, has become a trivial matter. Whatever hardships the world may bring—the Reorganization included—pales in comparison to the hardship of being without her. Yes, Earl has been hit hard, or rather he has allowed his pent-up feelings to break free. He has made no declaration to himself that opposing the Reorganization is to be abandoned, but it has been set aside in order to give his full attention to her. Together, perhaps, they will yet conceive of a scheme to stall its progress. Perhaps the FSA can be made to appear to be cooperating when its efforts are actually designed to fail. But that will come later.

The Day and the Hour: Finally

The trail through the woods follows the gently curving course of Gold Creek. So far he has not encountered another soul, but he expects that the police will be combing the area before long. Not too far ahead, Leila's residence is easily reached by means of a narrow trail that branches off the main trail and leads directly up the hill, away from the creek, coming out of the woods at the end of Deer Drive.

A siren goes by on Creek Street above, moving in the opposite direction. Earl estimates that they have found the stolen cruiser and will soon be on the trail behind him.

So far he has passed two benches and is looking for the third, that one which comes just before his turnoff. ... Yes, he sees it fifty yards ahead. If it bears the initials S+D carved into its backrest, it is the one.

That's it!

Earl Clark sprints up the hill, breathing hard while watching the ground to avoid exposed roots in the track. As the brush thins and the overhead canopy of tall evergreen trees gives way to bright daylight, the dead end of Deer Drive comes into view. Her apartment building, to the left, is the only structure on this bit of Deer Drive. He turns immediately into the garden behind the building in order to avoid being seen on the street.

In a casual manner Earl saunters toward her door, steps onto the deck, and taps the glass. The curtains have been drawn open, and he can see her bed. Her Bible lies open on it, and next to it the hat he left on Wednesday. Her personal phone is on the night-stand. Another siren goes by on Creek Street, but it barely registers in his consciousness because what he is seeing is telling him she is gone.

He taps on the glass again and tries sliding it open. It yields. Closing it behind him, he calls her name, but the evidence tells him not to expect an answer. He picks up his hat and puts it on, grabs the Bible, steps out, slides the door closed again, and walks stiffly back to the woods. He wants to find a place to hide, to mourn, and to die.

Mission Accomplished

Earl Clark tramps back down the hill and carelessly approaches the main trail. No one is in sight, and there are no sounds of approach. If he is to put any distance between himself and the pursuers, a side path would be preferable—quieter and easier than plunging through the wild wood with its thickets, mossy windfalls, and uneven ground. Suddenly, it occurs to him that they will be using dogs. Realistically, there is no practical means of escape. He must face what is coming.

Earl returns to the bench bearing the S↑-□ and sits down to await the inevitable. As we all know, this is contrary to his nature. He needs to be doing something—but what? A stupefying lethargy has come over him and is pinning him in place.

Forcing himself to think, he begins talking aloud:

"She wasn't there. ... She couldn't be there. ... She's no longer anywhere."

The evidence strongly suggested it, and now his gut assures him that the Rapture took place, and Leila was taken. How could he have been so mistaken? He remembers Carmen's note in his pocket, and he takes it out.

> Earl -
> If I'm gone, I'm gone,
> and you're wrong. Sorry.
> Hope they don't get you.
> - C.

He crumples it and puts it back in his pocket.

Earl opens the Bible at the ribbon, the page where Leila left it open, and *Samson* arrests his eye. It surprises him, for this is the New Testament, near the end of the Book. He reads:

> And what more shall I say? For time would fail me to tell of Gideon, Barak, Samson ... who through faith enforced justice ... were strong out of weakness ... refusing to accept release so they might rise again to a better life ....

He flips through the pages and notices notes done by her hand. He begins reading what she underlined, but does not get far before the sound of a panting dog's approach brings on a rush of energy and pulls him back to the present.

He cannot see them yet, but they must be close, coming up the trail on his right. Actions spring to mind: he could avoid being seen either by bolting back up the path to Deer Drive or by charging down into the woods toward the creek. Neither option would erase his scent, and neither would be silent. But there is no need to make a choice because the instinct to escape is powerless without the desire to carry it out, and his desire to escape disappeared with her.

Earl closes her Bible and folds his arms across it, pressing it tightly to his chest as if to absorb some solace from it or protect it from the enemy.

A German Shepherd on a leash followed by an officer from the local police department is seen coming around the bend. Earl recognizes them both. The man is Fillmore, one of the cops he forced to eat a cookie at the post office incident on Monday. Fillmore is reporting his discovery by radio:

"Dispatch, Fillmore. ... Clark is on the Gold Creek trail near Deer Drive. Over."

"Is he in flight? Over."

"Negative. He's sitting on a bench, the one with the S+D carved on it. Over."

"I'll have FSA send a car to Deer Drive."

"Roger. Fillmore out."

Earl sits still with his head bowed. The dog is straining at the leash and whining with Fillmore trotting behind. The Shepherd comes to Earl's feet and lies down, putting a paw on his shoe.

"I don't have to tell you you're under arrest, Earl. You look like you've had a rough morning."

"Do what you have to do."

"Put the Bible down. Turn around and let me have your hands."

Earl lays the Bible on the bench beside him and stands up, putting his hands behind his back. The officer slips the bands of the handcuffs over his wrists and tightens them.

"There's a lot of blood on the back of your shirt. Did you get shot?"

The sound of another siren comes from above.

Earl gives him no answer.

"Come on. We're taking the trail up to Deer Drive."

"I'd like to take the Bible," Earl says.

"We'll leave it there. Someone will get it tomorrow morning."

Earl plods up the trail, followed by the dog and the officer. A police car and the FSA surveillance car are waiting as they emerge from the woods. He is delivered into the hands of Officer Filstein of the FSA while Officer Fillmore and the dog get into the K-9 car.

"I'm going to have to blindfold you," says Filstein. "There's a lot of blood on your back. Are you in pain?"

Earl says nothing.

Officer Filstein takes a roll of tape off his belt, removes Earl's hat, wraps tape around the prisoner's head, covering his eyes, and slaps the cap back on.

"Surveillance, Filstein."

"Surveillance. Go ahead."

"I have Clark blindfolded and handcuffed. Heading up to Detention Suites immediately. Will be there in five minutes. Over."

"Roger. Will notify Cypher."

Although unable to see, Earl knows exactly where he is at each moment by the sounds and motions, and he knows he will be encountering Al Cypher when being admitted to Detention Suites, at which point he would like to deliver a swift strike to Cypher's jaw. He believes he can snap the band joining the handcuffs as soon as he has more freedom to move, but he would have to be able to see in order to deliver the punch. And it would not harm Cypher in any significant way. He wishes he were really Samson: he would bring down the FSA building with his bare hands.

The Day and the Hour: Finally

Cypher is emerging from the door as they arrive. Filstein stops, and Al comes to the car.

"We're having a little problem with security in the Suites," he announces to Filstein. "All the inmates escaped last night—or more likely this morning. Apparently the earthquake did something to the security system though I haven't found anything wrong with it yet. I'm going to have to put Clark somewhere else until we find the problem. The utility room around back is secured with an old-fashioned, reliable mechanical lock. I'm going to put him in there for now. As long as he's handcuffed and blindfolded he can't do any damage. Follow me."

Al Cypher gets into his own car, and Filstein follows. They drive around to the back and stop by a door at the center of the building.

"All right, Clark. Out you come," says Al Cypher. "Did you ever expect to see this day?" he asks Filstein.

"I won't guess how this will turn out, Cypher. But for your part, I would advise you to go easy on him."

"I happen to know what else he's wanted for," Cypher boasts.

Earl hears the sound of key in lock and of a door opening with a slight squeak. Al Cypher puts his hands on his shoulders and turns him toward it.

"Straight ahead," he directs his captive.

"There's nothing in there for him to sit on, Cypher," says Filstein.

"That's all right. He's tough."

"Can't you put him in one of the suites? He can't just walk out in his condition—not with you there."

"I don't want him around while I'm working. He can stay in here. It will do him good. Besides, he's all bloody, and I don't want him messing up the place. ... Coming to the threshold; step high."

Not wanting to touch Earl's bloody back with his hand, Cypher lifts a leg and shoves the seat of his pants with his foot. Earl stumbles forward into the room, and the door slams shut behind him.

Mission Accomplished

Whether due to the effect of his hat or of Cypher's foot, a surge of strength rushes upon Kenneth Clark. He strains at the handcuffs, causing the bands to sink into his wrists, but they remain intact. He moves his two hands over to his right side, and his right hand brushes against the end of a tubular railing. He stoops a little, sliding his right palm under the railing, and straightening his legs he pulls up hard with his right arm. The plastic cuffs cut through the flesh, causing blood to drip from his wrists. The connecting band stretches ... stretches, and snaps.

Using both hands, Earl tears at the tape that wraps his head and finally succeeds in peeling it off.

The room is small and without windows. An overhead light is on, controlled by a motion sensor. He is in a narrow space between railings that stand out a foot from the side walls. Behind him is the door by which he entered. The wall in front of him is covered with a chart showing the locations of the sprinkler-system valves and the locations of the hallway-blocking fire doors on each floor. He is in the fire-control room.

Rows of switches for controlling the valves and fire doors are on the side walls. Earl studies the chart. The building is symmetrical, right and left, with identical systems in each half. Each wing is equipped with four fire doors on each level. The switches allow the doors to be closed remotely from this room.

He reaches up with his left hand and flips the switch for the far door on the top floor and hears a faint rumbling as the heavy fireproof panel releases and rolls on its suspension track. As it slams shut, closing off the north end of the wide hallway, a slight shudder ripples through the building.

Lifting his left arm, Earl runs his bloody hand down the entire outside column of switches. The combined rumble of the massive doors makes a much louder noise; and as they slam shut simultaneously, he imagines there is a swaying and twisting in the upper floors. Immediately, before recovery is complete, Earl raises his right arm and runs his right hand down the corresponding switches on the opposite wall, and the outermost battery of heavy doors in the south wing crashes closed, inducing a slight twist in the opposite direction. Running his left hand down the next column of switches, the next column of massive doors is unleashed, delivering another impulse at the moment when the movement from the previous one is at its peak. Again with his right arm he releases the opposite column of doors, and they go slamming shut, augmenting the momentum of what has effectively become a twisting pendulum. Alternately releasing a column of doors on the left and then on the right, the building twists one way and then the other by ever-increasing degrees.

Additional loud noises—horrible noises—are occurring: noises that are not the sounds of slamming doors. The rhythmic twisting of the building has reached such an extreme that it has over-stressed some of the joints to the point where welds are breaking and bolts are shearing.

The building shudders violently when one of the upper floors breaks away and descends to the next level, pulling structural members after it as it crashes to the floor below. Having lost much of its support, the entire structure above collapses, plummeting down and adding its mass to the tumbling chaos.

There is no mistaking what the noises mean. Earl has observed that the fire-control room is surrounded by concrete walls that will provide him some protection, but an enormous amount of energy is in play which walls were not meant to with-stand. The screeching, scraping, and rumbling sounds are sicken-ing. The floor shakes beneath his feet, and the light goes out.

Something very heavy has come down and impacted the level immediately above. Debris and dust is falling into the fire-control room, and the sound is deafening. The integrity of the roof and walls surrounding him is failing. A fragment of the breakup above, something with sharp edges, penetrates the structure over his head and knocks him to the floor. As the walls of the fire-con-trol room continue to break up, material rains down from above.

Earl wanted to bring down Cypher's building. It is finished. But our modern-day Samson is no longer aware of anything.

Mission Accomplished

As Karen Martin rowed around the point and the downtown waterfront came into view, she hoped to spot Earl's T-bird parked at the newspaper building. But it appeared that the lot was empty.

The best place to beach the boat would be at the waterfront park where there was no bank, and that is where she was headed. It would land her less than a block away from the paper building and only two blocks from the police station.

She had tried contacting both of those places by phone; she had left voice messages but had not received a reply. Karen remained undaunted. If communication continued to fail, she would track him down somehow.

She observed cars on the streets, and the Lakeview parking lot appeared to be full. She had heard sirens, so she thought there would be a good chance of encountering a police car. Sooner or later she would find someone who knew something of Earl Clark's whereabouts.

After pulling the bow of the rowboat up onto the grass, Karen set out walking up Park Street toward First Avenue, looking for a police car to wave down. She knew the FSA patrol had been keeping track of him, and the town police would be able to secure for her whatever information she wanted. (Karen Martin, by virtue of her longstanding prominence, was known to everyone in town. She was, in her informal way, more powerful than the mayor—by the mayor's own admission.)

As soon as she reached First Avenue, she saw the K-9 police car approaching, driven by Officer Hyacinth Fuller. Fuller pulled over when she saw Karen lift her hand. Fillmore and the dog were in the back seat.

"Have you seen Earl Clark?" Karen asked breathlessly.

"They have him up at the Federal Building," Hyacinth answered.

"Why?" Karen demanded.

"He's been charged with assault."

"How did that happen?"

"Seems he had a little argument with an officer in the city. He was there last night; left this morning."

"Left of his own accord? If so they must have had an exciting time keeping up with Earl driving the T-bird," Karen declared (for she knew the car well, having owned it along with her husband before selling it to Earl).

"Well, he came back of his own accord. I don't want to shock you, but I must tell you he was driving a stolen car—a cruiser belonging to the city police force, as a matter of fact."

"Oh no! I've got to talk to him. Can you take me up to the Federal Building?"

"You bet. Climb in." Karen squeezed into the passenger's front seat made narrower by Hyacinth's ample form.

"How is it that you're on foot?" asked Fillmore from the back seat.

"Beach House Road is jammed up with parked cars. A bunch of people disappeared from there this morning."

"We're still trying to find out who is actually missing," said Hyacinth Fuller.

"It's all the church people, isn't it?" Karen asked.

"Doesn't seem to be," said Fuller. "There's something else going on. Apparently it's not what anyone thought it would be."

"Where did you pick up Earl?" Karen inquired.

"He was down on the Gold Creek Trail, sitting on a bench," said Fillmore. "He didn't resist when I arrested him."

"That doesn't sound like Earl at all," Karen objected.

Presently, Officer Fuller was calling ahead on the radio: "Al, I've got Karen Martin with me. We're heading up the hill. She wants to see Clark."

"He's not in the Detention Center. Go around to the west side. I'll meet you there."

"What's up with the Detention Center?"

"There's a little security problem. I've got Clark where there's no chance of him escaping."

Hyacinth drove directly to the back of the building where Al Cypher was waiting, standing with Officer Filstein. While Karen and Fillmore got out of the car, Hyacinth lowered her window and called out to Al Cypher:

"You were telling me the other day how secure your jail is. Were you just going by what you were told, or did you actually check it out yourself?"

"Oh, I checked it out, all right," Al Cypher answered, smiling.

"Did it ever occur to you that those boys got taken in the Rapture?"

"No, I can't say that it did."

"Wasn't Pamela Evens in there too?"

"She was."

"And she's missing as well?"

"The place was empty when I checked in at 8:30."

"And you found no signs of tampering with the system?"

"No."

"What's the matter with your brain, Cypher?"

"Until I'm sure they got out that way, which is extremely unlikely, I'm not going to trust the system. Clark is in the fire-control room, handcuffed and blindfolded. It's right over here."

"I want you to take him out of there right now. Put him in one of the suites and make him comfortable," said Karen Martin.

Al Cypher made no reply. He simply shrugged and walked to the door of Earl's prison, fumbling with his keys.

The dog in the back seat of the K-9 car barked.

"Hush!" said Hyacinth.

"What's that noise?" Filstein shouted to Cypher.

They all stood still for a moment, listening. Al Cypher looked straight up. From his vantage point, quite close to the building, he saw the vertical lines twisting perceptibly.

"Get back! The building's moving! Run!" he shouted.

While Karen hesitated, Cypher jumped into his car, Filstein jumped into his, and Fillmore slipped into the K-9 car next to the dog. All three cars sped to the far side of the parking area.

"Come, get in the car," Hyacinth shouted to Karen, opening the door for her as soon as the car came to a halt. "Something could explode." As there was nothing she could do, Karen ran away from the building when she heard unmistakable sounds of its distress and claimed her refuge beside Hyacinth Fuller.

A horrendous screech and groan accompanied by snapping and smashing sounds met their ears. Some of the windows were popping out and others were shattering. Panels plunged to the ground, and with a deafening, ground-shaking roar the upper part of the building descended on the rest like an accordion being squeezed shut. Only the top floor remained with its windows intact, having come to rest at about the level of the former third floor. An acrid odor filled the air as the wreckage settled. Grinding noises and hissing sounds continued to escape the rubble.

Cypher, sitting in his car, knows he must wait until the ruins have ceased their shifting and then make an attempt to rescue Earl Clark. It looks fatal for Earl though. Everything that was on the first floor appears to have been mashed and flattened when the floors above came down. He motions Filstein to lower his window.

"I never did trust that building," he shouts. "It was supposed to withstand the big one, and it couldn't take a little bump."

"How do you explain the delay?" Filstein shouts back.

"It was too flexible. It never took much to make it sway. I guess somethin' broke during the quake and then it gradually spread. I don't know. **Whoa!**"

The ground shakes violently; the cars bounce; the heap that was the FSA building is seen to be sinking into the ground, the earth having opened to swallow it.

"It broke through to the mine!" Cypher shouts to Filstein.

The whole mass of ruin is dropping down, making hideous, hollow sounds as the pillars under it buckle and it descends into the cavernous hollow below—dust shooting up around it as it descends into the earth. It comes to rest with its roof level with the parking lot, antennas rising up like masts on a sunken ship.

If you, even you, had known today the things which make for your peace!
But now they are hidden from your eyes.
Luke 19:42

Chapter Seven

Slow to Believe

By nine o'clock several cars had appeared in the parking lot at the front of Grace Bible Church. Evidently the pastor had been wrong, and no Rapture had taken place.

But the pastor was late.

Some folks were waiting in their cars while some had gotten out and were standing on the wide walkway leading to the front door. Among them were Richard and Richelle. Richard tried the door and found it was locked; then he turned around and smiled.

"I was sure glad to see the pope come out on TV this morning," he said in a loud voice.

But apparently no one else felt like talking, and no one offered him a reply. Perhaps no one knew what he meant.

"I hope Pastor Adam gets here soon," said Lucinda.

No one replied to her statement either, for no doubt everyone shared that same hope but now felt it slipping away.

By 9:30 nearly everyone had gone back to their cars to wait.

One young man—his wife was not with him—slammed his car door angrily and sped away, sending gravel flying.

The walkway in front of the church was deserted but for a woman who stood with her head bowed and pressed against the door. She was weeping. Richard, who had gone back to his car with Richelle, returned and attempted to comfort her. Finally, she turned and allowed him to escort her to her car.

No one seemed to notice that a number of the plants that had been growing near the front door were missing.

The last car left the parking lot at 10:30. From then on the parking lot in front of Grace Bible Church remained empty, and the church door remained locked.

The Day and the Hour: Finally

*H*omer Foster slept in after his late night out. Fearing that his friends had awakened his parents with their loud laughing in the driveway, he had let himself quietly into the house. It was four o'clock. If they had no knowledge of when he came in, he would be able to tell them the noise had kept him awake too. He tiptoed to his bedroom and went right to sleep.

At eight o'clock, Humphrey jumped onto his bed and awakened him. He admonished the dog and went back to sleep. It was ten o'clock when he woke up again—too late to attend Mass.

At the foot of the stairway he paused to look at his mother's painting. He had noticed it there by the moonlight coming though the window of the door when he tiptoed by it. He wondered why it was there.

Humphrey followed him into the kitchen where he expected to find something that had been left for his breakfast. The kitchen was clean. He opened the dishwasher. It was empty.

He ran back up the stairs and looked into the girls' bedrooms. Hannah's slippers were by her bed where she always kept them while she was sleeping, but the covers were thrown aside as if she had gotten out of bed quickly for some emergency. Holley's bed was neatly made, and none of her clothes were on the floor. Humphrey stood behind him whining. Homer tore back down the stairs, and went to the garage. Both cars were there.

"No! Mom! Dad! Where are you?" he cried.

He skipped down the back stairs and checked the back yard. Then he ran back upstairs and knocked on his parent's bedroom door. Hearing nothing, and fearing the worst, he opened the door. The bed clothes were in place. The silence was eerie.

Just then Humphrey opened his mouth and panted, letting him know he was right there with him. The boy fell to his knees and put his arms around the dog, buried his face in the animal's fur and bawled. He had been assured by his priest that God would never take his family away and leave him on his own.

The doorbell rang.

Slow to Believe

fter leaving the church, Richard drove slowly, undecided where to go. He and Richelle had risen early and had finished breakfast by 7:30. They were watching the news and waiting for the fateful hour. Richelle wanted to go outside in case Pastor Murphy was wrong about the quantum time thing and they would actually rise up like balloons. She didn't want to have to deal with the ceiling of the house and whatever difficulty that might lead to. So they went out into the back yard and stood in a spot where they would not be seen by the neighbors.

At precisely eight o'clock the earthquake made them look up. But there was nothing to see.

Richard, like many others, thought the quake was probably the extent of it and that if anything more significant had happened it would take time before the full story would be told. They went back into the house and found that the earthquake was being reported in a news, but nothing more as yet. Apparently it was felt everywhere at the same time. He finished the breakfast dishes while Richelle went to get ready for church.

Richelle had prepared herself to accept either outcome. It was a habit she had developed and perfected over the years. The ability to look at anything from more than one viewpoint had become a mainstay of her life. Her education in the liberal arts broadened the narrow horizon that she had received from her parents, and while in college she was encouraged to consider multiple approaches to answering any question. It became second nature to shift to an alternative viewpoint whenever a difficulty arose. She found it easy to agree with anyone because she had the ability to discern the suppositions upon which the other person stood. This technique extended even to her private feelings. If she found herself in uncomfortable territory, she simply shifted to another, like a person owning several homes who alternates her place of residence according to the season. When she found godly literature boring she would pick up a humanistic novel; they were two worlds with two messages, both equally valid.

The Day and the Hour: Finally

The concept of the Rapture had its intriguing aspects and its troubling aspects—like the other articles of the religion she subscribed to. When it came to a troublesome issue, she simply switched to her skeptical shoes and enjoyed taking a little walk as an unbeliever. If she happened to be in the company of a believer during one of those times, she was able to speak as a believer while maintaining her current state of unbelief. It was like a person owning a residence in the north but currently living in the south speaking as a resident of the north only when it gave an advantage.

This morning she had been an unbeliever but spoke as a believer. When the Rapture did not occur she was not only not surprised, she was happy that she had chosen the better viewpoint for the occasion. Richelle got through life this way with little difficulty. She used this technique to motivate herself to do whatever she wanted to do with grace and finesse. She was respected and admired by all who knew her. She spoke well of everyone and everyone spoke well of her. And her house was always clean and orderly.

Richard knew approximately how long Richelle would be taking to get ready, and desperately wanting to make sure the Rapture had not taken folks away, he got into his car and drove down Creek Street to the Lakeview because he knew there was a gathering of the Lakeview church planned for this morning. He found the parking lot full and the restaurant empty. It was the most eerie moment of his life. Still, there could be other reasons why they had left.

He went back home and waited for his wife to finish getting ready for church. While doing so, he looked for his Bible and then remembered he had put it on the shelf at church for the UN pickup tomorrow. He was restless, pacing the floor. The ultimate answer would come when they went to the church and found the others there. No one had been there yet when he drove by, but it was a little early. If many were missing, especially if the the pastor did not show up, there would be something to worry about.

"Why did we get left behind?" Richelle asked, as they drove away. While she had prepared herself for this possibility, there was a consequence: it was no longer possible to be a skeptic, and that part of her had suddenly become worthless. What was left was like half a person. She had relied so much on ambivalence that she felt she was now squeezed into a tight little place with no room to maneuver. Her world had shrunk. The Rapture had taken away her unbelief. It was like God had slapped her hand and told her to sit down and listen to him only.

"I wasn't sure it would happen," Richard admitted.

"They're having a grand celebration up there," Richelle mused bitterly. "What a party that must be. Everyone feels young again. People are being reunited ...."

There was a long pause during which neither of them spoke.

"We could go to the Lakeview for brunch," Richelle suggested.

"No. It's deserted. I already checked it out while you were getting ready for church. Nobody was in there: no cooks, nobody; just an empty room—empty tables with dirty dishes on them."

"Oh," Richelle muttered, and she fell silent.

Richard wanted to complain aloud but kept his thoughts to himself:

The "empty room"—that has an eerie sound. I hate the way this turned out. Most of those people weren't even baptized. We've been faithful church members all our lives and look what we get for it. What a lousy setup.

Cool it, Richard, it's just a story.

I don't care if it is just a story, you irony monger. It doesn't feel very good to be here. What do we do now? I bet you don't know either.

Listen to your wife.

That's not funny.

Look, Richard, you're just a figment of my imagination. I'll make you whatever I want. I doubt that anyone believes you're real anyway.

Give me a break. You're not God.

To you I am. You played your little predictable part well, I'll have to admit. I enjoyed getting to know you even if you are unreal.

I bet you don't have the hairs of my head numbered.

You don't have any hair.

Yes I do.

I never said you did.

Do you mean to tell me I've been going around during the whole story without any hair?

Of course you have. That's the way I thought of you.

How disgusting.

Just keep your hat on.

Now quit messing with me! I don't wear hats on Sundays; you should know that, and I don't care about hair. Why did you make the Rapture happen? I thought it wasn't a sure thing.

Nothing else would work. Scripture can't be broken. It had to happen.

Is it over for me? Or do I still have a chance?

Yes, to be sure.

I mean, will I make it when I die?

I'm not telling. You have to figure that out yourself.

All right, that does it. I'm an atheist.

I need your help tomorrow night.

What for?

The vote at the City Council meeting.

I'm not on the City Council.

Yes you are.

You never said I was.

I hardly mentioned city government.

I noticed that. I thought it was odd.

It would be a story of its own.

What is this vote about?

To make an exception in the horse-shoe ordinance for the Burns House. I want to get the property deeded over to the community for horse-shoe tournaments.

You had better talk to the mayor.

I am the mayor.

"I might have known."

"Let's go home," said Richelle. "I'll fix us some soup. Why did you say, 'I might have known?' Who were you talking to?"

"The person who wrote us."

"Was it Harold? It sounds like something he would do. He seemed to know what would happen."

"It was a female voice. I think it was Claudia. I'm mad at her. She likes to play God."

"All novelists do."

"But they don't mess with their characters the way she does. She has no right to do that."

"I suppose it makes it easier for her to accomplish her purpose."

"Yeah, well, she needs more practice. She couldn't even remember Simon's last name."

"I missed that. What day was it on?"

"I don't know. It was back there somewhere."

"What *is* his last name?"

"How am I supposed to know? It wasn't mentioned."

"Why don't we pick one?"

"That would be too bizarre; no reader would buy that."

"Why not? The story already has a lot of odd things about it. It's like a Christmas tree with cute and clever and crazy objects hanging all over it."

"Yeah, I know. We're just tinsel strands hanging out here on our little branch."

"Suddenly the shiny balls on the next branch are gone," Richelle said, continuing her metaphor.

"Some of them weren't so shiny. And they were all rather simple, if you ask me."

"You have to start somewhere when you take down the tree after Christmas is over. You start with the glass balls because you have places prepared for them so they don't get broken."

"Only because they're more fragile than the rest."

"I thought they were nice. Their beauty was in their reflections." (Her habit was to speak well of people. I am a bit proud of Richelle, I must admit.)

"Which is the same as saying they weren't very substantial; they didn't have any real shape or character of their own. Whoever beholds the tree sees his own face in those ornaments."

"At least they had surnames. She didn't bother to give us one."

"Careful. She might blot us out of her book." Richard laughs at his unexpected cleverness.

"I wonder if the neighbors will let us have our dog back."

"At least we had faith enough to make arrangements. That should have counted for something."

"Corrie and her husband didn't make any. They thought their dog would go with them. ... I wonder what happened to them."

"We passed them going the other way."

"It will be interesting to find out whether any pets are actually missing," said Richelle.

"Ha. Maybe our dog went without us. I didn't see him this morning."

"He is—or was—a pretty good dog. ... Richard?"

"What!"

"I just remembered something."

"What?"

"We're to take the Foster kids in if anything happens to their parents."

"So?"

"What if ..."

"Yeah, we'd better check on Homer."

"They had a dog too."

"What's that?—that rumbling sound. Look, the Federal Building must be on fire!" Richard exclaimed.

"I thought we could see it from here. I'm sure we used to be able to see the top three floors at least," Richelle observed.

"That's dust, not smoke. The building collapsed!"

Slow to Believe

Officer Al Cypher takes out his phone as the plume of dust drifts away to the southeast. I am only guessing, but I think probably he is not sorry that Earl Clark was inside the building when it collapsed. (I'm not guessing.) He is trying to contact his boss and gets no response. Her phone's location indicator is active, showing it being at her home.

On the spur of the moment Cypher decides to pay her a visit and deliver the news in person. He drives around to what was formerly the front of the building, exits the parking lot, and speeds down Hill Street the back way, leaving the others to wonder why he left without announcing his purpose.

Arriving at her apartment building, he notes that her car is there, which he takes as evidence that she is home. He rushes in through the main entrance, finds her door, and rings the bell.

Remembering protocol, Cypher unclips his radio and calls the surveillance supervisor.

"Surveillance, Cypher."

"Watchman here; go ahead."

"Where are you located?"

"At the Lakeview where Clark abandoned the car. Unfortunately, he took the key. Over."

"Did you see that the building collapsed?"

"Yeah. So much for the quake-proof design. Over."

"It's worse than you can imagine. It broke through into the mine, and the whole thing got swallowed up. ... Over."

"You mean the whole building dropped into it?"

"The whole building went to hell. I'm trying to find the boss. I'm at her place right now. I believe she's home because her car's here, but she's not answering her doorbell. Over."

"Where's Clark?"

"He was in the building when it collapsed. It happened fast. I didn't have a chance to get him out. Over."

"That's too bad. I suppose he had the key on him."

"No doubt."

"Well, it gets him out .... I mean, now you've got a chance. Over."

"It'll save the FBI some trouble, and I won't have to explain. ... Yeah. Do you think I've got a chance? I hope so. But we need to find her. Over."

"When they picked up Clark, he was down on the creek trail below Deer Drive. Fillmore said he had a Bible, which could be hers. I figure he was up to her place. Check the back door. Over."

"Clark wasn't known for packin' a Bible. ... Stand by."

Al Cypher goes around to the back of the building and finds the door unlocked.

"Surveillance, Cypher."

"Go ahead."

"Back door is unlocked. Over."

"If you don't get a response, go ahead and search the place."

"Roger."

Al Cypher bangs on the door and waits. He slides it open.

"Leila!"

Stepping into the bedroom, he notices her phone on the bedside table. He finds nothing of significance in the other rooms.

"Surveillance, Cypher."

"Go ahead."

"Nothing's amiss here. There's no sign of a struggle or foul play. Still, you need to put out an urgent missing-person search order. Over."

"I'm short of personnel. Hooper and Snooper are missing."

"Are we getting help from the town force?"

"Affirmative. They found our cars, parked side by side with nobody around and no bodies. And get this: The parking lot at the Lakeview is full, but nobody's inside. There's a sign on the door saying, 'Believers only.' Apparently, they met for breakfast. Over."

"No kidding? I feel like we're in one of those old End-Time movies. Did anyone check the churches?"

"A few people were hanging around Grace Bible Church when I went by, apparently waiting for Murphy to unlock the door once more. Over."

Al Cypher laughs. "That's funny," he says. "... Sorry; it just struck me that way. It looks like they were right, but what good did it do 'em? Over."

"Those are the hypocrites. I thought they all were. At least they still got a building—nothing a locksmith can't fix."

"It'll take more than a locksmith to fix ours. It'll set the Reorganization back a couple years."

"I'd say more like seven, minimum. It'll take a while to clean up the mess. Figure five years just for an impact study. What are you gonna do, Cypher?"

"Do you have any pull with Petunia?"

"A little."

"Do you think she'll have some openings?"

"I figure Daisy is gone. Maybe Daffodil too. Over."

"That leaves her Violet Farmer, Poppy Fields, and Peony Forester besides Fillmore.

"Don't forget Hyacinth Fuller."

"Oh, yeah. ... Would you put in a good word for me? She thinks I'm an idiot for not figuring that the inmates got taken in the Rapture—or whatever it was. I still think Pamela Evans got someone to let 'em out. What do you think? Over."

"Are there any clues to support that? Like, did she leave any personal belongings behind?"

"I noticed her purse and phone are still in her suite."

"You are an idiot, Cypher!"

"But you must allow this day is unusual. I'm generally on top of things. I really would appreciate it if you'd tell Fuller that."

"At a time like this? We gotta look out for ourselves, Cypher."

"I thought you were my buddy, Watchman. Over."

"I'm as good a friend as you'll ever get, Cypher."

"Hey, things are starting to work out for me."

"Yeah? Just because you got rid of Clark, eh?"

"I don't have to worry about him being with her, wherever she is; that's for sure. Over."

"Don't be too sure. If they were right ...."

The Day and the Hour: Finally

"There's no use waiting up here for something else to happen," said Hyacinth Fuller. Where would you like me to take you?" she asked Karen.

Officer Fillmore and the police dog had gotten out of the car and, along with Filstein, were patrolling the area while staying well clear of the ruins which continued to emit noises and vapors.

"You can take me down to the park. I'll row back home."

"I could take you to Beach House Road, and we could drive in as far as possible. The walk to your place from there I don't think would be very far."

"Then I'd be stuck without any transportation."

"You could walk the beach to town if you had to."

"Isn't the creek fenced off?"

"On the south side only, and there's a good chance you'll find a way through it. We've given up trying to keep the fence intact."

"Still, I'd have to swim across the creek," Karen pointed out.

"Not this time of year. You can wade across and not get wet above your knees, honey."

"No, thanks. I'll row my boat back. But it's good to know there's another way out besides hitchhiking."

"Does it seem strange to you...?" asks Hyacinth. "I mean, does it seem like a minor thing that this building collapsed?"

"I guess it does to you. Why, do you suppose?"

"Well, people are missing! Earthquakes happen and buildings collapse once in awhile. But people don't disappear into thin air every day. I never took the Rapture seriously enough. I didn't exactly disbelieve it would happen, but I never got comfortable with religion. I knew I was missing something that might be important, but I was afraid if I got involved in churchgoing I'd risk losing my job. I felt I was where I was supposed to be—and I still do. I love being a cop! ... But today is so, so strange."

"It seems strange to me that Earl Clark is buried somewhere under that rubble," said Karen. "Oh, there's Claudia! I need to talk to her. Thanks for your offer. I'll hitch a ride with her."

Are you unaware that
all we who were baptized into Christ Jesus
were baptized into his death?
Romans 6:3

Chapter Eight

Aftershocks

*T*his morning I went to the Lakeview, timing my arrival to be just before the Hour. I knew they were meeting for breakfast, and it would be the surest way to obtain a first-hand observation.

You see, most of the characters in this chronicle are real, so I have little control over what they do. Although there are no perfectly true biographies in these pages, they do represent people who live or lived at one time. And no one invents great events.

One thing you can count on is that the most bizarre characters are *not* the ones I made up. Regular people like Richard and Richelle I made up in order to give the story a degree of credibility. (If all your characters are bizarre, it feels strained and unreal to the reader.) When I looked for people in this town who were unremarkable to use in that way, I couldn't find any, so I had to fabricate them. Does that make sense? I know it's a contradiction, but contradictions don't bother me anymore.

I really wish I didn't have to make up characters. As every novelist will understand, even the purely made-up ones take on a free will and sooner or later do something that's embarrassing. I'm constantly having to reign them in, and if they don't cooperate and turn out badly, then it's my fault! So I much prefer writing about what has happened and what real people have done.

Of course, I didn't take the Rapture thing seriously at first—I painted a fairly accurate picture of myself in that—though I made a good case for it. (It's one thing to write about a subject: believing what you write is something else.) But as the week went on I nearly became a believer.

The Day and the Hour: Finally

When I arrived at the Lakeview, only one parking spot was left. I went in quietly and waited by the door, standing where Al Cypher stood last night. No one saw me come in. They were all kneeling on the floor with their faces down on their arms or bowed over their folded hands on the seats of the chairs. There were audible murmurings. I was a little uncomfortable, feeling like an intruder—indeed I was an intruder. But I thought it was important that I be there—just in case. If something did happen, I needed to be an eyewitness, I thought.

I recorded what I saw as well as I could. Yes, I swear they did disappear at exactly eight o'clock. But there are things that cannot be put into words. I left immediately, drove home, and spent the next hour in my closet, weeping. When the ground shook, I thought it was the end of the world. The noise was unlike anything I had ever heard. It rattled my house much as an earthquake would, but the sound was like a dozen train wrecks all at once. I dashed outside and saw that the Federal Building was collapsing. I waited until I thought it was safe, and then it seemed to happen all over again. When I couldn't wait any longer I dove up there and got the report from Karen Martin.

After taking Karen down to the park where she had left her rowboat, I came back up to my house and wrote that silly thing about Richard and Richelle.

I'm really broken up about Earl. I have my own ideas about what made the building collapse, but I'm going to find out more about that building before writing it up; then I'll insert it in the story where it belongs.

I nearly forgot: I need to pick up Harrietta's painting from her house as I promised I would. I hope she isn't there; then I won't have to display her amateurish thing in the Gallery. But I'm afraid she will be there. I would not want to predict what she will say and do if she is! Too bad Richard and Richelle weren't real. You remember they were going to check for Homer and the dog. Richelle would have had some calming effect on Harrietta. I could always count on Richelle.

Aftershocks

*R*ev. Kirby Amill went ahead and delivered the sermon he had written last week while working under the assumption that no Rapture would occur. Since any other out-come would be extremely problematic for him, he had decided to ignore the possibility. Then after his unsavory encounter with Adam Murphy on Thursday in which he was shamed for denying the necessity of the Millennium, he decided that in the event that some sort of departure did occur, he would cast it as an unholy event. The proof would be his congregation remaining intact.

You can be sure that Kirby will not go that far, however, when he is faced with the reality of the event.

As of the moment he stepped to the pulpit, he believed that the prediction had been a failure. He had checked the news at 8:30. As expected, there was nothing substantial being reported. There were interviews with people who were disappointed that nothing had happened. There were replays of segments of ser-vices in mega churches that revealed no disappearances. During the subsequent analyses, it was mentioned that the unusually low attendance was attributable to Rapture hysteria. So far there were no confirmed cases of missing persons. It was suggested that the earthquake was what the Rapture dreams had actually been about. What made the quake worthy of this unusual warning was the fact that it was unique in the history of earthquakes, being felt all over the earth. Since no geophysical model could accommo-date it, scientific opinion was that both the warning and the quake had no cause—just as the universe had no cause.

Following that bit of preliminary investigation, Kirby had attempted to call Adam Murphy—to offer his condolences. But the pastor was not answering his phone, which was not surprising either. The embarrassment that Adam must be feeling would make a recluse of anyone—at least that was what he told himself.

He avoided getting into a conversation about what did or did not happen this morning as people came in before the service began. The FSA building had not collapsed yet at that point.

The Day and the Hour: Finally

The title of his sermon was "Dispensational Dangers."[1]

Seeing as we are all here this morning, we have a clear indication that God has not singled out a particular belief system for his approval as some of our brethren would have had us believe. We must renew our trust that the Almighty steers a steady course and that we need not fear new revelation. Until the time is ripe, we shall continue our work on earth, looking forward to that day when peace will unite our brothers and sisters around the planet, cooperating for the good of all God's children—including every creature great and small.

I'm glad to see that we have visitors this morning. Perhaps you have come because your church's pastor decided to take this Sunday off, which surely is a good thing to do now and again. We welcome you to First Presbyterian and hope that you enjoy your time together with us this morning.

This has been a tumultuous week, has it not? I know that some of you found it entertaining. For others it was an unsettling and confusing experience. No doubt, advantage was taken of our brethren in their sincere but mistaken belief, and for that we should be offering them our consolation and help in healing their wounds.

You may have watched the news this morning, as I did, mostly out of curiosity about how the networks would cast this less-than-excitiong hour of non-fulfillment. Their conclusion, that apparently nothing happened, was not a surprise to us, of course.

Some of you older folks will remember midnight on December 31, 1999 when the world was poised on the brink of disaster, according to many so-called experts, as computers would fail to perform properly due to their inability to handle the year 2000. I was reminded of that non-event this morning. No doubt there will be some people who will take advantage of this to "disappear"; no doubt there will be stories and rumors propagated by pranksters. But our faith is not to be taken hostage by purveyors of sensation.

---

1. Kirby was very kind to give me a copy of it. You will see later how he struggled and failed to maintain his denial of the Rapture.

On the other hand, we have to admire the faith of those who were convinced that the so-called Rapture would indeed occur and were willing to demonstrate their faith in a tangible way. Those large churches that had televised services were certainly putting their reputations on the line—that is, those that were promoting the Rapture and not against it or agnostic about it. I believe there was a sigh of relief everywhere.

This is a potent reminder of the dangers of literal interpretations of Scripture. The history of religion is littered with the ruins of movements that collapsed as a result of taking things out of context and applying them too literally.

Those who mistakenly expected to be translated to heaven this morning were following a particular way of looking at the Bible, called dispensationalism, which attempts to reconcile the conflicts caused by overly-literal interpretations. The dispensationalists assume that God administers different programs at different times and places. Unfortunately, the outcome is an emphasis on exclusivity rather than unity. Ultimately, it downgrades Christendom or the church to a temporary phenomenon on the earth, making it an interlude between two dispensations centered on Judaism.

This is at odds with evolution. In reality we find that the best elements of religion always survive and develop into something greater. We can look forward to continued fusion of the most enlightened strains of religion from all cultures. The premillennial dispensationalists would have us believe in a future throwback to the religious rituals of ancient Israel. Of course, educated people have a hard time accepting that concept. Nevertheless, in religion there is no limit to what people will believe —or say they believe. It seems to be part of the game.

The doctrine of the premillennial Rapture is a case in point. Something was needed in order to terminate the present dispensation and make way for the next. Thus the Rapture was "discovered" as the missing link. In order for certain prophetic utterances in the Old Testament to be fulfilled literally, they found it necessary to remove people of the church age, as they call us, from the picture so that a new dispensation—which is a glorified return to the old Jewish dispensation—could take place. It takes a great deal of effort to overcome the plain truth that having people just disappear is a preposterous proposition. Yet in the realm of religion it seems that any ruse works as well as another—for a while.

This morning I would like to point out the three basic problems with dispensationalism.

First, it gives us a provincial God. In the history of religion, deity among primitive peoples was always seen in the context of a particular culture. This is really an artifact of limited knowledge about the world. Today, almost everyone is aware of the vast numbers of people in the world, their varying cultures, and their peculiar traditions. It is no longer acceptable to view God as favoring a particular race or culture. Yet that's exactly what the dispensationalists do when they insist that Jews have a special standing in the divine economy. This may have been excusable in pre-Christian Israel. But there is nothing more obvious to the student of history than the fact that the Jews as a race, or Israel as a nation, fulfilled their purpose in giving birth to Jesus Christ. The complete destruction of Jerusalem in year 70 of the common era speaks clearly of this fact.

Secondly, the dispensationalist's hermeneutics suffers from insufficient attention being paid to the cultural bias and nationalism that is found throughout the Old Testament, particularly in Deuteronomy and the prophetic books. When we allow nationalism to be what it is, we are not minimizing the divine origin of the Scriptures. Rather, we are giving due recognition to the humanity of the authors and the customs of their times.

What our liberal orthodoxy boils down to is an honest, informed approach to reading the Bible. The dispensationalist errs greatly in this respect, taking scriptures that are clearly poetic hyperbole as if they were literal prescriptions. You have to smile at some of the things they come up with when they try to take these writings literally. But again, this is religion, and you can get people to buy almost anything.

The third problem I see with dispensationalism is that it is a late development. The Rapture, as it is understood by dispensationalists, was essentially "discovered" in the nineteenth century by John Darby. It stretches one's credibility to believe that great theologians who formulated the foundational doctrines of the Christian faith somehow missed seeing what has so lately been discovered. I must admit that there is a certain attractiveness in the way the dispensationalist fits things together and makes literal interpretation almost plausible. If one puts aside the obvious absurdity of the provincial God who talks like an Israelite trying to justify his imperialistic dreams, it appeals to a certain type of individual. It even had a following among some early Presbyterians. But I daresay we have moved beyond that.

While the novelty of dispensationalism faded a century ago, and it's brief day of respect in scholarly circles is long gone, it continues to draw life from the Rapture. Is there anything quite as dramatic and romantic as that fable? You can carry out your Christian duty by giving the poor man a house on a street corner, and he will have physical comfort and the privilege of paying taxes. But how does that compare with giving him a ticket to heaven that could transport him at any moment to a mansion in glory and the privilege of dining with the King? The house may satisfy the needs of the body, but the story of the Rapture is a myth that satisfies the soul. More than that, it crosses the line between dream and reality; it is a myth you can believe in.

So I don't want to be one to pronounce its demise prematurely. I suspect it will take more than this latest failed prediction, as dramatic as it was, to do that. If the past is any guide to the future, the Rapture will live on in the imaginations of men and women as long as they believe in heaven.

After the sermon, offering plates were being passed when noises of the FSA building collapsing disrupted the organ's "Onward Christian Soldiers." Those who remained seated put their money away and nervously passed the plate.

The Day and the Hour: Finally

Rowing home after having witnessed the collapse of the Federal Building at close range, Karen Martin has one thing and one thing only on her mind: she is forming a plan to rescue Earl Clark, assuming, of course, that he is still alive.

When Martin Construction Company was excavating for the foundation of the Fitness Center, a ventilation shaft into the abandoned mine was uncovered. Ken Martin spoke to Earl Clark, who was the owner's representative, and they decided to leave a way into the mine from inside the building. They designed a concrete cover for the shaft, which became the floor of a large utility closet. Later, after the building was completed, the part of the closet where the shaft was located was walled off, and a door in the floor was opened. Earl made a simple elevator consisting of a hoist and a car sized for two bodies, which allowed them to get down into a tunnel of the mine. They spent some time exploring that tunnel and others, and they mapped out the hazards they encountered. They found the distance to the main cavern, from which most of the ore had been taken, was less than 100 yards. This was before the FSA building was built on that spot.

Earl Clark, Ken Martin, and Karen Martin were the only people who knew about this though several rumors have it that the Martins took out various amounts of gold during the construction of the gym. Now Karen hoped to bring up more than treasure. She knew where to find the map that Earl and Ken had made, and she had a set of keys that would allow her to disable the security system, get into the Fitness Center, into the utility closet, and through the locked door into the room where descent to the mine was possible—or was possible at one time. It had not been used since Ken and Earl did their exploration.

After tying the boat to the dock, Karen rushes up to the house and begins collecting and checking off the items she plans to take: a bright portable light, boots, gloves, helmet with light, a mask against dust and fumes, a first aid kit, a bottle of water, ropes, an ax, a hack saw, a tarp, and a large backpack to hold it all.

Aftershocks

Karen asked me to see that the abandoned automobiles on Beach House Road got towed away as soon as possible, and I made the necessary calls.

But Karen is now ready to go and the roadway is still blocked. As she walks impatiently toward the string of abandoned vehicles, it occurs to her that some or perhaps all of the drivers left keys in their cars. If so, she may find one with enough energy in its battery to get her to town and up to the Fitness Center.

And so she does.

Of course the parking lot is vacant today. She parks near the door and has no difficulty with the keys. She switches on the light in the secret room where the hoist and elevator car are as they were after Ken and Earl finished their exploratory descents. The car is a cage-like affair with a plywood floor, constructed of pipes welded together. In the corner of the room is a small pile of ore showing bright streaks of mineral.

The control for the hoist is at the end of a cable that hangs inside the cage. On the wall of the room is a small breaker box with its door open. Karen switches the breaker for the hoist to the "on" position. Then she steps up into the cage and tests it by pushing the upper button briefly. The hoist groans and the cable goes taut. She holds the button down longer to let the car rise two or three inches off the floor before releasing it.

Under the car is a heavy steel door that must be opened. Channels in the floor perpendicular to one of its sides suggest matching rollers on the bottom to the door. A cable runs from that side to a pulley on the wall and up to a hand-operated winch. Karen finds that the winch turns easily and the door comes smoothly on its rollers, causing a gaping black hole to open below the cage.

Though only a few inches separate the edge of the car's floor from the edge of the hole, it takes all the courage she can muster to step in and lower the cage slightly to make its floor even with the floor of the room. She steps out, puts on the boots, helmet, and gloves then shoulders the pack but decides it will be easier to heave it into the car first, which she does and then steps in.

The Day and the Hour: Finally

Karen would like to take a deep breath at this point, but a dank odor she first noticed when the cover began to roll away has become much stronger. She gets the mask out of the pack, puts it on, and switches on the helmet's light.

According to the map, the distance down to the floor of the tunnel is 55 feet. The hoist is slow, taking some seconds per foot of descent.

Once descended fully into the shaft she watches the rough rock wall rise slowly in the spot illuminated by her headlight. It seems to be taking a long, long time—far too long. Then suddenly the wall is gone and she is hanging in the horizontal tunnel. A half minute later the bottom of the cage contacts something with a metallic sound, and Karen releases the button. She expected this, for the map shows rails running down the middle of the tunnel. But she did not expect to hear other noises: apparently parts of the collapsed building are still shifting and settling.

Karen is not sure that the car did not rotate as it descended, and moreover she is uncertain about the direction it faced originally. The FSA building (that is its remains) is located north of the Fitness Center. According to the map that Ken and Earl made, the tunnel slopes downward gradually in that direction. She digs the bright light out of the pack and shines it between the bars of the cage, poking the beam in several directions. The tunnel is supposed to be 15 feet wide here, and so it appears to be. The door of the cage is conveniently facing the direction in which the tunnel appears to be descending.

Karen steps out onto loose rocks in the space between the rails and shines the light down the length of the tunnel. The sides and top are rough and jagged. The map shows it making a bend to the right some 50 yards distant, then running straight for another 50 yards before meeting the main cavern where she expects to find the wreckage of the building and hopefully Earl Clark.

She gets into the straps of the pack and adjusts it carefully to make sure it is balanced before proceeding. Obviously the footing will be treacherous. The tunnel was not built for foot traffic.

Picking her way carefully, Karen succeeds in getting to the place where the tunnel begins to bend to the right. As she approached the bend she was surprised to see light in the tunnel ahead. Now as she rounds the bend, the wreckage of the building comes into plain view, illuminated in places by light from above.

Noises other than the hissing sounds of water escaping from broken pipes—the occasional scraping and screeching noises—are much louder now, but there is no danger of being hit by a falling object as long as she remains within the tunnel. She wonders if anyone had thought to shut off the water main—or perhaps it was left on intentionally to reduce the chance of fires spreading.

Karen halts a few feet from the point where the roof of the tunnel vanishes. In front of her is a mound of earth that apparently came down with the building. The floor of the cavern appears to be flooded. She is wearing high boots, for she anticipated encountering water, but she did not appreciate the difficulty of ensuring secure footing in water. She ventures closer, stops again, and scans the wreckage with the beam of her light.

There is some space on the left between the debris and the rough side of the cavern which might allow her to proceed toward the place where.... She did not expect so much water. She shouts: "Earl!" and listens. The hissing sounds seem extremely loud.

It could be that the water is not deep, but to get to it she will have to get around the mound of earth. Climbing over it would be treacherous. She calls again: "Earl! ..."

Karen slips the pack off and unlashes the ax, thinking she can make use of it head-down as a walking stick, but it proves to be awkward. Taking only the light, she makes her way along the cavern wall but after a short distance finds the passage blocked by slabs of broken concrete. Carefully, she picks her steps and wishes she had brought the ax. Clipping the light to her belt, then bending over and using her hands, half crawling, she gets up, over, and around some of the obstacles but then faces water right up to the cavern wall. A shower of earth falls from above just in front of her.

"Earl! ..." Hissing sounds are saying she must accept defeat.

The Day and the Hour: Finally

But Karen Martin is determined. If Earl is alive she will find him and bring him out somehow. If he is dead she will search through the rubble until she finds his body.

She turns around and retraces her steps back to the tunnel. If she had brought a shovel it might be possible to clear some of the mound between the end of the tunnel and the cavern floor. But what if the water is too deep for wading? As she looked down when standing on the pile of broken concrete, it appeared dark and murky. Even if it is shallow, there will be no way to see obstacles unless her light penetrates to the bottom. She must find out. She decides to risk it and begins climbing over the mound.

Getting to the top of the heap is not her concern, of course. Rather it is the danger of loose material sliding under her feet as she attempts to descend the slope to the water's edge.

But she cannot see the other side from where she stands. Perhaps something solid is on the far side, or perhaps the pile of loose material does not extend quite to the water.

She did not notice before starting that bits of soil and scraps of roots and plants are constantly falling from above like light rain. But instead of harmless drops of water, they are sometimes clumps and often stones. Yet she ignores the likelihood of being struck by something heavy enough to harm her and proceeds to climb the slope, causing small slides with every footstep.

From the top of the mound she discovers a narrow outcropping of solid rubble at the water's edge. But now: does she dare descend to it on the unstable slope and risk causing a slide that might carry her down and on into the water?

As she stands trying to decide how to descend the slope, an overhanging fragment of the building breaks away and plunges into the water, causing a wave that splashes over the outcropping and comes partway up the slope, proving that the water is deep.

Karen feels like crying. She calls out once more: "Earl!" and sits down on the spot where she stood on the heap of earth, letting debris rain down on her helmet and shoulders and legs. "Earl," she appeals softly, "—Earl, where are you?" as tears flow.

The fruit your soul lusted after is gone
and things that were dainty and sumptuous are dead to you
and men will not find them at all.
Revelation 18:14

Chapter Nine

Missing Persons

*E*ven after finding strong evidence that his boss among others—including his own son—had disappeared, Al Cypher was unwilling to acknowledge that it had happened, and he set out to find her. It gave him a direction in which to focus his anxiety and a means of quieting the anger that threatened to make him do something even less defensible.

As a first matter of business he checked the number on the car bearing LEILA on its license plate that was parked by her apartment building. Why? To make sure it belonged to her? (He would not be able to explain why he did it, and neither can I.)

Then he began patrolling the streets as if by some chance he would find her walking the sidewalks. (He told himself she had to be somewhere, and that was his only justification.)

So starting from Deer Drive, Cypher began exploring the series of dead-end residential streets that intersect Creek Street.

On Porcupine Place he encountered a scene suggesting domestic violence. He knew the house. It was the residence of Ed Child, a fireman employed by the local department. A chair lying upside down in the yard evidently had been pitched through the window, judging by the size of the hole in the glass. Cypher lowered his window and listened for sounds that would confirm the nature of the violence. Mrs. Child was screaming at her husband, accusing him of murdering their two children. (That would be Eddie and Jennifer. Jennifer was famous for her skill in model-car racing. Eddie was famous for his tantrums at the food market.) The last thing Cypher wanted to do was intervene in this scene, but when he heard the word "murder" he had to act.

The cop was admitted by Mrs. Child who volunteered the full report without him asking for it. From where he stood, not far from the entry door, he saw that the house was in extreme disarray. Mrs. Child was angry about the Rapture. The Children disappeared, she said. She said she was mad at heaven for doing it to them. Ed Child spoke up and blamed his wife for not responding to an invitation to learn about the Rapture.

"*Me? You* blame *me?*" yelled Mrs. Child. "*You* were the one that threatened Harold Foster!"

"Who threw the chair through the window?" Cypher inquired.

"I did," said Mrs. Child. "I told my husband that's what I would do to him if I could. If he'd listened to Philip Evans and Harold Foster when they came by to warn us this would happen, I wouldn't have lost my children. By his negligence they're gone forever—like being dead. What's the difference? They're gone!"

"She's dangerous," said Ed Child (who is physically fit as a fireman must be—and twice her size). "You need to lock her up till she calms down."

"What do you expect of a mother who's lost her children?" demanded his wife.

"I could arrest her," said Cypher, "but presently I've no place for it, and I'm on another urgent detail. Come with me, Ed."

"Am I under arrest then?"

"You are if that's what it takes. Come on, let's get out of here."

Cypher turned and left the house with Ed Child on his heels.

"You're not getting out of this alive, Ed Child," his wife screamed after them.

"I'm looking for my boss," Al Cypher announced as he swung the patrol car around and sped away from the scene of the crime.

"What? Did she disappear too?" asked Child.

"I've been unable to reach her; that's all I know."

"Is it possible she was abducted along with the rest of 'em?"

"It is, of course," replied Cypher, "but I'm not accepting that until I've exhausted every other possibility."

"She's following us!" Ed was looking in the rear-view mirror.

"Leila's following us?" exclaimed Cypher excitedly. "She must have seen me looking at her car."

"No! It's my wife! My wife's following us."

"Oh. ... Too bad."

"Yeah. Too bad is right. Her weapon is deadly."

"What is it? She's going to get a speeding ticket in a minute."

"Her car is her weapon! Be careful. She'll use it!"

"Look, I'm not about to be chased by an angry woman."

"It's our only hope. You can outrun her."

"No way. That's not how things are done."

"Then stop and get behind a tree with your gun out."

"That's not an approved procedure, Ed."

Cypher stopped just after turning at the intersection, activated his flashing lights, and backed up to block the street."

"Get out!" shouted Ed Child as he flung his door open and bolted. Seeing the danger, Al Cypher did the same and narrowly avoided being hit as Mrs. Child, who came on fast and plowed her small vehicle into the side of the cruiser, causing her air bags to inflate as the front of her car crumpled like a paper cup.

Dripping blood from her face, Mrs. Child squeezed out of her wreck and attacked her husband. Ed Child grabbed her arms and held her in a hammerlock as she screamed curses and threats.

Cypher produced a roll of tape and handcuffs, and the two of them managed to gag and bind the raging woman.

"Security, this is Cypher."

"Security."

"Ah. ... I need a tow. ... Ah. ... Two. .... Two disabled vehicles here. Corner of Lake and Park."

"Hi, Dad! What happened to Mom?"

Eddie and Jennifer had come running up from the park.

"Where have you been?" demanded their father.

"We wanted to make you think we went up in the Rapture."

"You .... What made you do that?"

"You said it would never happen. So we knew you wouldn't really think we went to heaven."

The Day and the Hour: Finally

Jake wanted to know who went and who got left behind. Though he was surprised by the disappearance and impressed that it had happened some time around eight o'clock—as far as he could tell—he was far from being sure it was what the preacher had said it was. He knew the reputations of all the members of Grace Bible Church, so he was curious about the residue. He wanted to see if there was evidence that the departure selection had been on some nonreligious basis, such as physical and mental fitness, which would be expected if the abduction had been carried out by an exploratory mission sent from another planet.[1]

He had a hunch that Ned, or "Brother" Ned as he preferred to be known by his church associates, would have been left behind if the aliens possessed accurate intelligence about physical fitness. On the other hand, Ned was a long-time member and officer of the church; therefore, Jake figured he would not have been overlooked if the Rapture had been what it was billed to be.

So Jake stopped first at the house where Brother Ned lived. He rang the bell and waited. He knocked and waited. Thinking it likely that Ned had been taken, he was turning to leave when the door opened and Brother Ned stood there in his bath robe.

"Hi Jake. What brings you by?"

"I ... I'm surprised you're here."

"Oh, are you? It's nice of you to say that. I might say the same for you."

"Well, then we're in this together."

"Whatever 'this' is."

"Mind if I come in?"

Ned stepped aside and mutely swung his arm as if to sweep a path for the visitor.

"I take it you were as surprised as I was," said Jake.

Brother Ned sighed. "I suppose so," he said, and he yawned.

"What do you think will happen next?" Jake asked.

---

1. Jake could have saved himself the trouble of trying to support his doubts if he had observed the floor more carefully at the house where Laura had dwelt.

"What do you mean?"

"What does the Bible say will happen next?"

"Nothing."

"I mean, isn't there an antichrist supposed to take over the world?"

"I don't know anymore."

"Your wife? ..."

"She's gone."

"Are you sure?"

"Look. ... Look at this here." Ned grabbed Jake's arm and pulled him into the next room to examine a certain chair. There was a strange smell and a coating of fine dust everywhere.

"She was there, in that chair, and then it was like she caught fire and literally went up in a cloud of smoke."

Jake put his arm across Ned's shoulders, and they stood in silence for a few seconds. Finally he said, "There are no words for it. ... Can I do anything?"

"No. Nobody can do anything now. We're done for."

"You heard about the FSA, I guess."

"Heard what?"

"About the building collapsing."

"I heard noises. Was it bombed?"

"No. Apparently the quake damaged it."

"Good thing it's Sunday. Was anybody in it?"

"Earl Clark was."

"Earl Clark? How did that happen?"

"He had just been arrested. Al Cypher stuck him in the Fire Control room."

"And the building came down right after that?"

"Shortly after that as I understand it."

"Earl Clark brought it down," declared Brother Ned.

"What makes you think that? He was handcuffed and blindfolded."

"That's proof that he brought it down. I always wondered about him."

"I don't follow you, Ned."

"He did it for his girl ... you know. Now she doesn't have to cooperate with the Reorganization."

"Leila Labaki? She's gone too, apparently."

"Well, that's a double setback for Cypher then."

"Where do you get all this?"

"Ever hear of Samson?"

"Of course. You mean Samson as in Samson and Delilah?"

"Doesn't Clark remind you of Samson?"

"Well, I don't know, Ned. I don't know that much about it."

"I'll show you what I mean."

Ned picked up the Bible that was lying open on the floor near his wife's chair and shook off the dust. "Samson was a judge in ancient Israel. His story is here in the book of Judges. Chapter sixteen, I think. ... Here it is. Read this:"

> And Samson called to Yahweh, and said,
> "O Lord Yahweh, remember me, I pray, and strengthen me, I pray, only this once, O God, that I may be avenged of the Philistines for my two eyes."
> And Samson reached out to the two middle pillars on which the house rested and leaned on them, one with his right hand, the other with his left.
> And Samson said, "Let me die with the Philistines." He pushed and strained with all his might, and the house fell upon the lords and upon all the people that were therein.

"I see a slight similarity," said Jake, "but you'll have to explain a few things to me. Who are the Philistines? And how many of them were in the FSA building when it came down?"

"The Philistines were Israel's enemy. Samson was ordained by God to subdue them. To Clark, the enemy was the Reorganization, and by wrecking their facility he set them back a few years in this town, wouldn't you say?"

"But nobody besides Earl Clark was killed."

"I think some are out of a job—like the bosses and the staff they hired to get the Reorganization set up."

"Well, okay, that's interesting," Jake allowed. "Maybe he had explosives on him."

"Do you think so? No, Cypher isn't that stupid. Clark pushed it down with his bare hands. He broke the handcuffs and found something in that room that could damage the building. Or maybe like Samson he prayed, and for him it was enough."

"Who am I to say you're wrong?" Jake conceded. "I wouldn't object to calling it a miracle after what happened this morning."

At that moment the doorbell called Ned away, and Jake looked at the time. He was anxious to check out a few more suspects in town before getting away himself."

It turned out to be Leonard, another bereaved member of Grace Bible Church, come to see if Brother Ned remained. Neither Ned nor Jake vocalized their surprise at seeing him.

"Ned has a theory about the FSA building," Jake announced. "He thinks Earl Clark played the part of Samson in the Bible."

"Ha ha. I think so too," said Leonard. "Like Samson he was foolish enough to let a woman turn him over to the enemy."

"That's the first time I ever heard someone call Earl Clark a fool," objected Brother Ned.

"You don't think it was foolish of him to get in a compromising relationship with the FSA boss?" returned Leonard. "I'm told she put the cops on his trail yesterday after he broke free of her FSA surveillance detail. Then like a fool, he came back as though he hadn't meant it and let them arrest him without any kind of a struggle."

"Claudia thinks he was in love with her," Jake offered. "That'll make a weakling out of a man."

"She had to get rid of Clark because he was opposed to the Reorganization," continued Leonard. "She's as bad as Delilah was or worse. No doubt she was promised a reward if she could deliver Clark to the FBI. Samson finally got his strength back and retaliated at the end, but it cost him his life. So I agree with Ned that we have a virtual reenactment of that story."

"There's only one problem," said Ned. "Leila's gone."

"Right," Jake confirmed. "And that adds to my suspicion that the Rapture wasn't quite what it was assumed to be. If it was heaven calling true believers home, how did she get included?"

"Where either of you at the Friday-night service?" Ned asked. "Well, if you had been there you would have seen something surprising. About twenty FSA employees showed up, and I hear most of them got baptized yesterday."

"And she was at the service too?" Jake wanted to know.

"No, she wasn't there, and I don't know why. But she was responsible for them being there."

"So you think she had a change of heart?" said Jake. "I guess that's possible. But then why did she get the cops out after him last night and this morning?"

"It could be she was in love with him as well," suggested Ned. "If she knew she was leaving with the Rapture, she would want him near and try to get him to join her."

"Actually, she was supposed to be delivering him to the FBI," said Jake. "So her plan had been to get him arrested and hold him in custody here. That would give them time to work something out. But you could be right too, Ned. If she was converted on Friday, it was either a perfect solution or perfect disaster, depending on the timing and Clark's decision."

"Funny thing about Earl Clark," said Ned. "His best friend was Pastor Murphy, and people like Leila Labaki that spent time with him usually become Christians. But yet he wasn't one himself."

"I heard Chester Matthew was taken," said Leonard.

"That's what I mean," said Ned. "And nobody cared as much for this community as Earl Clark did. I always admired him because of that. And now we have him to thank for keeping that hellish Reorganization at bay for a few more years."

"It would be just like him to sacrifice himself in order to accomplish that," said Jake.

"You know what I think?" said Ned.

"I can't imagine," Leonard muttered.

"I think if she hadn't been taken, Earl would have failed."

Missing Persons

After that Jake excused himself, and having endured enough nonsense for today he almost abandoned his little project; but on his way back, as he drove up Howard Street, he remembered Archie and swung a left on Second Avenue. He had intended to include Archie in his survey. If he found Archie at home, it would be a strike against his abduction suspicion: Archie was an intelligent professional, a talented architect—world renowned in fact—and the type of person that would interest visitors from another universe. The compensation to Jake would be a sane discussion about the impact of the departure and what the future might hold for everyone else.

It turned out that the renowned architect was at home, and Archie seemed happy to see him. Archie said he had just gotten back from his second visit to the ruins of the FSA building.

"What caused it?" Jake inquired.

"Well, I'm not sure," Archie replied, "but I've ruled out so many things that I have to believe there was a fundamental flaw in the design of that building."

"You weren't involved in the design of it, were you?" asked Jake rather facetiously.

"No, fortunately I wasn't. But I might have made the same mistake. These days there is so much reliance on computer modelers that you lose your grip on principles and end up trusting the wisdom in the computer model they put together. But with all its intelligence, the computer is liable to overlook a flaw that in the old days we would be alerted to by our gut feelings."

"What was the flaw?"

"I believe the shell had a dangerous sway mode due to insufficient stiffening against torsion."

"You mean like twisting?"

"That's right."

"It always did twist," Jake confirmed. "In a strong wind from the south you could feel it twisting on an upper floor. I never experienced it myself, but I heard about it more than once."

"If a structure lacks restraints or sufficient damping, its natural frequency can be excited by just the right repetition of force such that it enters a mode of swaying or twisting back and forth like a pendulum. But it's not at all clear where that force came from this morning."

"Do you think the earthquake had something to do with it?" asked Jake.

"That's the only thing on the table," said Archie. "It's possible that the earthquake weakened the foundation. There were pillars down to the floor of the mine cavern that supported the girders in the foundation. It's conceivable that a difference in lateral motion between the foundation level and the level of the cavern floor might have caused a pillar or two to buckle. It could have happened in such a way that it caused the foundation to twist or rotate slightly, and during the ripple of torsion to the upper floors some structural connections got stressed to the breaking point."

"Then why didn't it fall immediately after the earthquake?"

"It must have sat there with something broken, say a floor support at the top level, with a significant mass gradually sagging and then breaking loose after a period of time. After that a cascade of events caused the building to collapse which put a sudden load on the columns below and causing one to buckle then another until finally the unsupported mass plunged down into the cavern."

"I thought all buildings were designed to withstand strong earthquakes," said Jake. "The one this morning was so slight. We've had them much stronger. I can't imagine it damaging any normal structure."

"I know this sounds crazy, but there was a new earthquake-proof design theory pioneered in that building. By its extreme flexibility it was supposed to endure any quake short of a chasm opening under it. But apparently they failed to properly analyze the twisting mode. The motion that people noticed on the upper floors was normal. The built-in flexibility that allows such motions also reduces stresses."

"Could there have been an oversight in the construction—something missing or poorly made?" Jake asked.

"Quite possible, quite possible indeed," Archie agreed. "If so, some evidence of it could be in that wreckage. But then who is to blame? Inspectors? Contractor? Foremen? Welders? Suppliers? I would hate to see the finger of blame pointed in their direction. Ultimately, the architect is to blame either for the design or for not having called out errors during the construction."

"I'm surprised you're able to look at it that way."

"It's because I'm retired. When I was involved in a project it was like I was God because I always got blamed for everything. I thought it was unfair then, but I didn't complain. I just carried a lot of insurance."

"Off the record, who do you think is to blame in this case?"

"I don't know. The computer modeling was extensive and went through many iterations, balancing probability of quake damage with the economics of construction. The location was a bad choice. It was dictated by someone who thought the symbolism of a dominating location was worth the extra cost of the foundation and support pillars. But I will say that this case will improve modeling and prevent this kind of vulnerability being built into future buildings."

"Do you have something to contribute to that, being early on the scene?"

"Yes. I've gotten as much detail as I can out of the FSA officials who witnessed the event, and from that and my own inspection I'll be writing a report. I'm not sure what I'll do with it yet, but there are several possibilities."

"What about the cleanup? How long do you think it will take?"

"It will be difficult and dangerous. They'll have to proceed slowly, taking it out piece by piece and never knowing when something will shift. It will need some engineering and planning. It could take a year or more to remove all the material."

"I think the site should be abandoned and left as a monument and an attraction, leaving it available for future study."

"That's not a bad idea," Archie agreed. "Where do you think a replacement could be located?"

"I own some acreage by Four Corners I'd be willing to sell."

Archie laughed. "I'm sure you wouldn't donate it. But there's a multitude of possibilities if the architect has any imagination. For example, the building could be an archway spanning the existing site. Your monument could even remain under it."

"That's an interesting idea. Would it be wider and lower?"

"Yes. If you want a tall, noticeable building, it could be a mini-spire with the added advantage of having a small footprint."

"What about parking?" Jake asked. "That takes more space than the building does."

"In the city, where there's an efficient alternative, that wouldn't matter so much, but you're right: here we still need parking."

Archie was looking out his window at the back of the old Howard Hotel (which currently houses my art gallery).

"They could take the Gallery spot by eminent domain," he said. "And it could incorporate a parking garage that would help relieve the downtown parking shortage."

"Don't let Claudia hear you say that. How about this: let them take my office at First and Hill. There's nothing between that and the Catholic Church that's of much value: a second-hand store, a barber shop, and the empty storefront."

"Are you planning to go out of business, Jake? You look pretty young to be retiring."

Jake laughs. "Yeah. The bottom just dropped out of the market. Here's another idea: south of the park where the Fosters are located. Soren and Sylvia, I mean. That would be perfect. It's between the downtown area and the commercial district. It's right on the lake. There's plenty of space, enough for the building and generous parking. Unfortunately, they still live there, I'm sure."

"Why would they not still live there?" asked Archie.

"They weren't serious church members, you know."

Archie looked perplexed. And then it dawned on Jake that Archie was assuming that the Rapture had not taken place.

It will come to pass at that day ...
that and the priests will be astonished,
and the prophets will wonder.
Jeremiah 4:9

Chapter Ten

Time to Get Serious

*D*ottie and Dale attended the eleven o'clock service at their church as usual. No one said anything about the Rapture, according to their pastor.

I interviewed Pastor Don and he gave me his analysis. I think he was being frank. I believe he was still in shock. At first he resisted evaluating the part he had played and the influences he had had on others. He was unable to face what had happened to him personally. I had not known him well, and I would not have detected anything abnormal about his words and demeanor if I had not been expecting to find a man in the throes of denial. It seemed obvious to me at the outset that his mind had partitioned off its feelings. He was performing at a survival level, though the clues were few until we got further into the discussion.

"No, it was a normal service," he said with a dismissive shrug of his shoulders. "I took the position implicitly that the Rapture expectation was a mistake, and we should be above criticizing anyone for having believed in it. Our Christian response was to forgive them and not bring it up. We all understood that without me or anyone having to say it."

"How was the attendance?"

"It was low, but that was inevitable and expected. No, I shouldn't say that. While some would be too disappointed or embarrassed to attend, others would be anxious to see who was missing. So I don't know. ... Some were taken."

"When did you learn what had happened?"

Pastor Don stared at the floor. I gave him time to answer.

"My wife disappeared," he said without emotion.

143

"Right before your eyes? Was she in the same room with you?"

"No."

Of course I didn't inquire further about that. "I'm surprised you were not taken yourself," I said, for I could think of nothing else that might engage his theology, which is the surest way I know of to get a clergyman into theory and away from the problems of real life. But it didn't work; he was unable to move in that direction, which I should have foreseen.

"I was ... well, I was sort of expecting it, and yet I wasn't. I knew there was no other reasonable explanation for the dreams. I had the dream myself, which I assume you know. But it was so far out of place according to my understanding that somehow it paralyzed me instead of engaging me. I ... well, I—"

"And so you were unable to acknowledge the event, and you acted as though nothing happened?" I wanted to ask him how he could do that, knowing that his wife had disappeared, but I didn't.

He nodded his agreement but offered no words in reply.

"Was there a discernible difference in the behavior of those who were there?" I probed.

"I saw few happy faces. But they were very attentive."

"Like they were waiting for you to say something?"

"No doubt."

"And you didn't?"

"I simply delivered the service I had planned. It was routine. Really, I could have done nothing else."

It was one o'clock when I called on Dottie and Dale. I had encountered Dale at one or two Council meetings but did not remember where he lived, nor did I recall having met his wife. What I had written about them earlier I had surmised from what Lucy, their daughter, had told me.

Dottie answered the door and invited me in. They had a news channel up on the screen and were eagerly waiting for the analysis they had not gotten from their pastor. Dottie told me they had assumed nothing had happened. Dale never took his eyes off the screen. I sat down and watched it with them.

Time to Get Serious

The cameras that had been placed in mega churches had cap-tured almost nothing. Nevertheless, they were rerunning the clips every few minutes. Commentators and their guests kept repeating that there was no known evidence of any disappearances. How-ever, the audio on those clips did catch what sounded like one clap of thunder in the background, and there was a slight shaking in the video, which most likely had been greater than it appeared, judging from the shake we felt here. The announcers accounted for this phenomenon by saying that a small earthquake had struck at exactly eleven o'clock, Eastern time—apparently everywhere at once, though they didn't point that out. It was reported as though the quake had nothing to do with the Rapture or else that it was all that the so-called Rapture had amounted to.

In one segment, a reporter was shown standing by a graveside in a cemetery with what appeared to be an open Bible and quoting the "dead in Christ will rise first" from First Thessalonians 4:16 over and over again. The camera showed him walking among tombstones and pointing to those with crosses on them, proving that there had been no extracting of bones from graves. And that, he pointed out, was proof that the Rapture had not occurred because the Bible said the dead would rise first.

In reality there was plenty to report. There had to be, judging from what I knew had happened here. For one thing, they might have mentioned that both the President and her Vice President were missing, which the Rapture promoters had been predicting would happen. The House Speaker is a rabid anti-Semite and totally inadequate for the presidency. Perhaps that's why they're now predicting a major war in Israel without giving any logical reason why it suddenly appears more likely today than it did yes-terday. It was announced that two rabbis are missing in Israel: two Jews unaccounted for makes the news! I think that was meant to imply that no Christians had been reported missing—and who knows? Maybe all the Christians over there are the wrong kind. Everyone in the church I belong to turned out to be the wrong kind. Well? Am I boasting about that? It feels like it.

The Day and the Hour: Finally

I saw no mention of the space signals having ceased. Jake tells me the picture is no longer scrolling through Scripture. Evidently, the masters of the media are attempting to lead everyone to believe that anything we observe or experience is a local event unconnected to any massive disruption such as the Rapture would have caused. There was, however, a report of a massive prison escape in Georgia. I don't know how that one slipped out.

The Vatican is announcing an ecumenical initiative—again—and I'm sure the timing is aimed at taking advantage of weakened Evangelical pressure—whether as a result of the removing of vocal opponents or the weakening of their credibility, I suppose doesn't matter. There is a new emphasis on the Mother of God as a uniting principle, and Muslim groups are on board because of that. Even Animists and Satanists were mentioned as having something in common with major religions. In that connection, a medicine man who approved of the terms of the initiative was interviewed. He added at the end that there would be no objection in his village because it was nearly empty. It was all very weird.

One thing, though, turned out to be accurate, and when I heard it I actually entertained a hope that Ernie and Enid did not get left behind. This bit of breaking news was that the cruise ship they were aboard went aground this morning as she negotiated a sharp turn in a narrow passage. Then Dottie got a call from Enid while I was still there, and you know the rest of that story. This was actually when I first heard about their ordeal. I haven't heard anything since, so I don't know if or how they got off the ship. I can't imagine Enid in a sling dangling below a helicopter.

After Dottie told me what Enid had said, I changed the subject and asked her how she felt about being left behind. We had gone into the kitchen to get away from the noisy TV. She looked at me with the most curious expression I think I ever have seen on the face of a woman. She was speechless. If you have read what I have written before about her, you know that Dottie is never speechless. She hadn't realized that there had been a Rapture. Whether she was glad to be left behind or not I couldn't determine.

Time to Get Serious

I t had been a good life, but it had suddenly come to an end because it was not good enough. Larry had failed to be what she needed, and she had left because of it—exactly as if she had walked out on him. No: worse than that because she left for another man. Jesus had taken her and rejected him.

Larry Link had been brooding since Lucy's departure three hours ago. Now the day was over, and it had gotten dark: it was late in Babylon.

He had been warned, and he had not taken the steps he needed to take. He could have preserved their relationship if he had been a responsible sort of guy. Now he has lost her and will have to go it alone.

He was far from an ideal husband. Could she have been glad to be leaving him?—a dreadful thought, yet at that moment it seemed plausible.

He had never imagined it would be this extremely painful if she ever left him. He would still have the dog, but now, suddenly, Junior seemed insignificant, like a toy almost. He had thought of Junior as being human—certainly as good or better than any human being for companionship. But it was a lie. Why had he persisted in something that was not true? He always knew it was half joke.

Why had she let herself go without him? Why did she let him carry on with his skeptical attitude about all things pertaining to God and the Bible? She must have known it would come to this, and she was not concerned enough about it to plead with him. Maybe she left him a note somewhere.

Larry got up and switched on a light. He searched her night stand and the dresser drawers and the pockets in her jeans hanging in the little closet and found no note.

How will he explain this to the authorities? Maybe Lucy was the only believer foolish enough visit the Great City. If he is the only one whose wife has vanished, they will accuse him of having disposed of her. However, that is a minor point. She is gone, and without her there is nothing to look forward to or to be afraid of. No more discussions. No more arguments. No meals together. No children.

Junior was looking lonely too, though he could not possibly have known what happened. The utter stupidity of the animal struck him for the first time. Last week Larry had vehemently protested that if Junior did not go to heaven, he did not want to go either. How idiotic was that?

Oh God, why did she have to go?

The discussion Larry had had with me Tuesday afternoon (prompted by his question about purgatory) came back to him.

I hope Lucy isn't in purgatory!

That awful thought returned, but thankfully Lazar's vision had replaced the fiery one. Larry hoped that it was true, but he would never know.

I wonder who else got left behind.

It was only a passing thought. Really he cared very little about that.

He had been pacing about the room. He returned to the bathroom again and looked for anything she might have left.

It couldn't be. It just couldn't be.

Saying that did not ease the pain in the slightest. He had made a horrible mistake, and his future looked very bleak.

Larry stopped his pacing and sat down on the bed. Junior knew something was wrong, and it showed in his cautious movements. He came over to his master and hopped up beside him.

"Lucy is gone," said Larry.

Junior lifted his ears as if he had not heard rightly.

"Yes, she's gone. Gone forever. It's you and me now."

Junior whined a little and looked up as if he could not believe what Larry had said.

"I said she's gone. We ain't got a woman no more."

Junior whined and really seemed to share his distress.

"God took her. He didn't want us. I didn't know this could happen. I really didn't."

*A*round half past one this afternoon, Rev. Veronica Sweet left her house on Parson Street and walked one block down the hill. There she hesitated briefly as she glanced up and down the street to make sure no one would see her—because she had stopped at the dwelling occupied by Fr. Murphy of Our Lady of the Lake Catholic Church. She knocked on the door.

Veronica had never called on the priest before. Indeed she seldom spoke to any of her neighbors. They moved in separate professional orbits that made neighbors virtually invisible. What compelled Veronica to seek Aaron's company today was the agony of having been so very, very wrong—and, making it infinitely worse, knowing she had *known* she was wrong. She brought with her a question for an excuse to be calling on the priest, but she really sought solace, not answers or advice.

That sympathetic company might be found on Parson Street where it never existed before was a reasonable expectation now that everyone had to go back to basics. The game had changed, and former lines of demarcation had become irrelevant in the wake of this morning's departure. Those whose investments opposed the Rapture had sunk like so many deflated balloons. It is disheartening enough to have an honest conviction overturned. So imagine having to face the truth that while you knew you could very well be wrong, you refused to admit it; you failed to acknowledge the multiple signs and warnings for what they were. I include myself in this. In retrospect, I think we were so overloaded with surprises we could not decide what to think about one before the next one came along. However that may be, any and all justifications are meaningless now because some of our neighbors welcomed the uncanny events as being in line with their expectations—after the first warning. That's what really set us apart.

Veronica desperately needed company. In her mind she stood at the edge of the abyss. She told me she was truly a basket case if ever one stumbled down the north side of Parson Street on two legs. You see, her daughter, Valentine, disappeared this morning.

The Day and the Hour: Finally

I assume she was in her mother's sight at eight o'clock when Valentine vanished though I have not pressed Veronica about that particular detail.

As you know, I like Veronica Sweet, and I had admired the cleverness of her art form—which I considered to be nothing more than that. I judged her vocation of selling imaginary real estate in heaven no different from my selling paintings depicting hellish depravity: both meet a need. What we offer may be more effective and economical than a course of psychiatric treatment—for the consumer, you understand. But she had been doing it for defiance of what she knew was true. I think she was a victim of her educa-tion.[1] She majored in defiance as did many of her classmates.

Veronica confessed to Fr. Murphy that one thing kept her alive: one bright object remained undimmed by the frightening feeling of being lost in darkness that enveloped her and loosened her grip on reality. Laura was her name. She explained to the priest that Laura had been a living saint whom she had befriended and who was now among the blessed residents of true heaven. She admitted that in her desperation this morning she had grasped the one thing within reach: she had prayed to her own St. Laura. Now she was here wanting to hear from one who prayed regularly to saints, about the propriety of requesting favors of a resident of heaven who had no seniority. She had asked St. Laura to watch over Valentine, or if that were not within the scope of her ability, to see that Valentine found company from home and to tell Valentine that her mother was thinking of her.

Fr. Murphy listened patiently and smiled. Veronica had come home. He reminded himself that there was much to be gained by steadfast service to the Institution of Christ, and here was a per-fect example. Who did heaven expect to take care of souls such as this if not servants such as he?—not that this one was unusual, for

---

1. So many of the younger ones are like that until they get their feet on the ground decades after graduation and find it is not only financial debt they accrued: they have to unlearn some things to get out of the academic hole. After that enlightenment some of them learn to navigate reality and find freedom to allow themselves to enjoy success.

the mother Church and her comforting Lady were constantly ministering wherever tangible elements were needed to support faith. This woman, who had admitted that her futile ministry had been draining her vitality, had come to the end of her resources a day too late. Given one more day she might have followed Laura's example, but she had been left behind and was devastated. What would be accomplished if *he* had suddenly abandoned his post? Veronica Sweet would be adrift in a sea of lonely regret with nowhere to turn for spiritual comfort. No doubt there would be more of this sort knocking on his door.

Thanks to the Rapture, Fr. Murphy told Veronica, she was now in good hands and in a place where she could begin to make her life count as a faithful communicant of the mother Church. He assured her that with careful counseling she would be accepted for baptism and become a joyful partaker of Holy Communion.

Veronica was speechless: the priest was a marvel.

A thought had came to Aaron at that point, which he did not verbalize but rather laid out before the Lord: he had known that his brother was right—that is, for him it was right; it was fine for his younger brother whose horizon was limited by the covers of his Bible. But his own faith welcomed the legacy of two thousand years of development which superseded the original documents in many ways. Was he wrong thinking this?—he petitioned the Holy Virgin too. If he had been wrong to minimize the authority of the Holy Scriptures and teach falsehood to others, would there be a penalizing layover in purgatory for him?[1]

Veronica had to turn her back on the abyss in order to marvel at the unperturbed confidence emitted by this promoter of ritualistic dogma. Yes, the priest's bold presumption was shocking. Merely because she had admitted praying to a saint, he had gone so far as to assume that she was ready to lay her future at the feet of the spooky goddess who claimed his prayers.

There was a knock at the door.

---

1. If you don't know it already, I'm a close friend of Fr. Murphy's. I heard about this directly from him.

The Day and the Hour: Finally

Without rising from his seat, Fr. Murphy called out to the visitor, commanding whomever it was to come in and join the holy remnant. He said "holy" with a wink for Veronica's benefit, and she wondered whether he had been completely serious. (She really did not know Aaron. If you do not know him well, you may not know that he is never as serious as he pretends to be, which to me is part of his charm.)

The visitor who obeyed the summons and opened the door for himself was Rev. Kirby Amill who resides next to Rev. Sweet on the uphill side. Dr. Amill was happy, though surprised, to see Veronica there, he said, because never before had he found reason to speak to her. (He omitted saying that he avoided doing so because of the absurd content and nontraditional mode of her ministry.) But now he felt drawn to fellowship with any and all clergy who shared the humiliation of being wrong.

"I knew we would meet one day," said Fr. Murphy to the newcomer. He remained in his chair, which the Presbyterian rightly interpreted as letting him know who held the senior rank.

"Have we become the ecumenical committee in town, then?" Dr. Amill asked in a tone that clearly said he was disappointed with his reception.

"No, we're past that. That was the old dispensation," returned the priest, and he grinned as he watched the reaction of the amillennialist for whom he supposed "dispensation" was a dirty word.

The formerly reformed minister grimaced. "If I've learned one thing, I've learned what a dispensation is," he said, aiming squarely at the target his opponent held up for him.

"Nonsense," uttered Murphy with a dismissive wave of his hand. "The disappearance was not in the providence of our God, you may be sure of that. So find yourself a chair, brother, relax, and join our neighborhood conversation."

The Protestant knew exactly what the Catholic Church's latest pronouncement on the "disappearance" was, and he doubted that anyone truly believed it. So he made no reply as he dragged a chair out from the table.

Veronica was not amused by this scene. She asked her neighbor if he had lost anyone in his family.

"No. I was fortunate," he said. "E.T.s generally leave us alone because we don't believe in them," he quipped and laughed.

"I heard you preached against dispensationalism this morning," said the priest.

"Word gets around quickly," Kirby said with unconvincing resignation.

"Wasn't that a bit embarrassing?" chided Aaron.

"Why should it be? Look where it got them."

"Where did it get them?"

"You tell me which world they went to. Yours is the church with the answers."

Veronica got up to leave. "I thought I would find a bond of repentance among us," she said, "and what I hear instead is petty bickering. I thought you would have put that behind you. Neither of you lost a loved one, so you carry on as though no one was seriously affected by what happened. I'm ashamed that I have to live on this street."

"Please sit down," urged the Priest. "We'll get over it shortly."

"Yes, I've been unconscionably rude," confessed Amill. "I did not know you had a loss."

"I would not call it a loss," Veronica shot back. "You seem to be in denial of what actually happened. It was more than a loss. For me it is the end. My daughter opened her heart to the promises of the Gospel only yesterday, and today she was assumed into heaven. I would have joined her in an instant if I had foreseen this. I was wrong, wrong, wrong! Wrong about everything that mattered, and so were both of you or you wouldn't be here."

The men were silenced. Veronica glared once more at each of them and walked to the door.

"Wait!" cried Fr. Murphy. "I want to hear more. I cherish sincerity, and you exhibit a thousand times more of it than we do. You're right: it's time we got serious and figured out what's real. While I cannot begin to feel the particular anguish in your heart,

I'm nowhere near as unconcerned as I sound. It's a cover-up, my dear. We men don't know how to speak our heart's truth in each other's presence. All we do is boast. So please stay. With you here we have some hope of being genuine. Yes, I repent. I've been wrong. My brother was right—very, clearly, obviously right. And I've been talking like a fool who doesn't know it." He crossed himself and looked to Rev. Amill for a similar response.

"I had a talk with Adam Murphy about this," Amill said. "I knew he could well be right, but he was so incensed at my aversion to some of the implications that he laid it on me pretty thick. I once was into dispensationalism, but then after it began to lose traction in the marketplace of theological thought, I decided it best to go back to the safety of my reformed roots before I suffered too much loss. I was not enough of an independent Bible scholar to judge the competing positions rationally, so I went according to what felt right. Obviously my feelings let me down, and I probably knew this could happen."

"You're both so far from facing reality it makes me sick!" exclaimed Veronica. "Look, we have a solid data point like nothing else since the rain lifted Noah's ark off the ground. From now on everything we think we know has to be built around this fact: some of us were taken to heaven and some of us were left behind."

"You're absolutely right," put in the priest. "I never could see the point in the Rapture, but now I'm forced to figure out what the point of it was. As far as I knew, if there was a purpose in it, it was to rescue faithful people from difficult times, and that didn't make sense because God's people have always suffered hard times; so why should this generation get special treatment?—you know. Now I have to figure it out, and I'm at sea with no rescue in sight from either the tradition I've known or the dogma I've studied."

Veronica remained standing, still glaring at them. "So you're at a loss because your doctrines don't cover this, and Dr. Amill apparently doesn't have the right feeling to help him sort it out. It may shock you, but I believe if Laura were here right now she

would have the answer. She had no theological training whatsoever and was largely ignorant of the Bible, but she had a simple
clarity of mind that was astonishing. Why don't we try approaching this as children and ask God to show us the way?"

"It could be that it's very simple," said Dr. Amill.

"Yes, in fact I know what Laura would say," Veronica added.
"She would ask a simple question. She would ask, 'What does God
need us to do for him in heaven that we can't do here?'"

Dr. Amill threw up his hands. "God really doesn't need us to
do anything for him," he declared.

"I don't agree with that," said Fr. Murphy calmly. "Maybe at
some high level in your theory, but we're done with theory. As
Rev. Sweet has said, we have this real data point, and it has no
place in your theology. So let's be like Laura and ask what God
might be doing with the people he lifted out of this life so abruptly
and what knowledge or piety qualified those particular ones that
the rest of us are lacking. Someone said it's a wake-up call, and
that's obvious. Now we have to wake up and figure out where we
went wrong."

"I can't believe you men," said Veronica, scolding them still.
"You never get out of yourselves, do you? My daughter was just
called to heaven, and she didn't know the first thing about ... well,
she knew the first thing—"

"And she accepted it without question, right?" asked the
priest.

"Of course she did. My point is, if she's in heaven without any
qualifications other than that, then why? Tell me how she fits into
this event that has been planned for ages when you two devoted
disciples didn't fit in?"

"God's elections are mysterious and always have been," pontif-
icated Dr. Amill.

"I don't buy that," protested the priest. "I'm sure you remember the parable Jesus used to explain what you call election: the
servant who invested his talents and reaped dividends was elected
to an administrative post over cities while the poor fellow who

carefully preserved his meager talent and failed to invest any of it got booted out and sent to hell."

"Well, yes, but you can't take a parable literally, of course," objected Amill.

"Then how do you take it?" Murphy asked him.

"I don't take it at all. I let it be there to remind me that I'm not to bury my Christianity—as our Lord suggested in another parable, to let my light shine."

"I'll tell you what the parable of the talents means in this case," said Veronica. "It's as though Laura whispered this to me just now. I heard her say, 'Emma has her reward.' Emma was Laura's daughter—or rather her sister's daughter in her care. Valentine is Emma's reward! And there's the answer I was looking for. Those two girls were called to rule over a city. Emma couldn't do it by herself, but the two of them together will be co-regents in the kingdom. They're soul mates—I saw that right away—and they're inseparable. ... What did I just say?—the kingdom? ... The kingdom of heaven here on earth in modern times? A universal kingdom? ... Yes, thank you Laura. We're talking about the kingdom of God when Christ returns to rule the earth. And that means Valentine will be here. I feel so much better!"

"You know what kingdom she refers to, Kirby," said the priest.

"Of course I know. But I'm not prepared—"

"No, you haven't been prepared, and neither have I been prepared. But the light has dawned, and now we must face the fact that we missed the point of everything. We were in the dark. But some were not in the dark, and they have gone on to collect their rewards and get their assignments—if you follow that line of explanation. I'm starting to see that what we received and taught about the purpose of life was comprehending almost nothing."

"Then are you telling me that was the reason for the removal? —to prepare them to be rulers of some kind in the Millennium?" Dr. Amill pressed the priest with a quizzical smile.

"Yes, of course. It makes perfect sense if you simply take the parable for what it says."

"And if I don't? There's a simpler justification for the imminent parousia: it's an incentive. It was an incentive to be serious about pleasing Christ in order to not be ashamed at his coming."

"Well, I agree with you that that *is* ultimate simplicity. But doesn't it amount to malicious deception if that's all it's for? I mean, if the day and hour of the return of Christ has been known to the Father for at least two thousand years, why would it have to be falsely advertised as being as likely to happen today as any day in the future? Isn't there enough incentive in the fact that one knows not the day and hour of one's own death? Isn't that the point you made use of in your preaching, not the imminence of a parousia?"

"Well, yes, of course. But at least in these times, when signs of the end have been fulfilled, it became an incentive to them."

"What signs do you refer to?" queried the priest. "Jesus warned against finding signs in wars and rumors of wars and earthquakes."

"And that the love of many would grow cold at the end," Dr. Amill reminded him.

"And what of that? That sign is deliberately vague and has existed somewhere in every generation. No, this Rapture thing has preceded any clear sign. You are left with no reason for the removal unless you accept what Rev. Sweet said: it must be that the folks who left us are supplying an important part in the divine plan—and probably being prepared for something. Office holders in the kingdom is a reasonable assumption. Whatever incentive there was in the knowledge that some might meet Christ in the air before his final coming could not be its purpose—any incentive was just an unavoidable byproduct, I say. Yet it had to be advertised in Scripture; otherwise, right now every one of us would have no reason to believe anything other than that a mass abduction by aliens took place this morning and they sucked up all the compliant types they could find."

Dr. Amill responded by folding his arms, and he said, "Then explain to me why God needs help governing cities."

The Day and the Hour: Finally

"Look, Kirby, this is about the day when the government of this earth *literally* rests on the shoulders of Christ. This is not my comfort zone either; the Second Coming was supposed to be the end of everything. But now we have to look at the doctrines held by those who were proven right, which I'm trying to do. Surprisingly, I feel certain that it was nonsense to hold that Christ's return had no great purpose. Think of it Kirby, if the world does go on under a godly government, millions of obedient and competent ministers will be needed. How else could it work? Do you think angels would be suited to deal with the nitty-gritty of human conflict? Now that I'm thinking about it, it seems quite obvious to me that the first wave of ministers under Christ will need special preparation."

"Have you forgotten the military campaigns?" asked Dr. Amill. "If you hold the kingdom to be literal, you also have a literal war on your hands to usher it in."

"Not my hands—"

Just then there was another knock. "Come in!" shouted Fr. Murphy as Veronica stepped back from the door.

The door was pushed open, and Pastor Russell Tarr from across the street strode in boldly as if he were accustomed to visiting the priest every day.

"Good," said Fr. Murphy. "Here's a man who knows about the kingdom. We're all commiserating about our failure to anticipate the Rapture, Russell."

"Would you mind if I use your computer?" Pastor Tarr asked, ignoring the question that had greeted him. "I need to look something up. We're getting ready to reopen the store."

"Go ahead. You know where it is."

Without acknowledging the other visitors, Russell left the room and disappeared into the spare bedroom Aaron uses for a library. They heard him close the door.

Fr. Murphy explained: "He's been over here before to use the computer. Witnesses were discouraged from going on the internet —actually prohibited at one time. Though the Uninet is relatively free of religious content or anything that might expose JW history, still Russell is afraid of losing some of his hard-won reward."

"Is he one of the 144,000?" Dr. Amill asked with a professional smirk.

"It's his hope. But let's get back to our topic before Rev. Sweet loses patience with us and takes away our access to Laura's clear thinking. I would like to know what the reason is for it. I mean this whole Millennium idea: what interest does heaven have in literally and forcefully governing the whole world—not to mention trampling down the opposition in order to get it all started? I've always considered that this world is the Church's responsibility, and if there's any trampling to be done it's up to us. We know that Satan is doomed, which means the Church *will* be victorious. After that there is no point in keeping this planet—which will be thoroughly polluted, worn out, and used up by then. Mother earth will have served her purpose. She will be dead or dying and fit for cremation while her billions of children who received the sacraments will migrate to the New Earth and enjoy Christ, his mother, and all the saints forever."

"If I may say so," said Veronica, who stood with her hands on her hips, "your argument fails because you have not established that your Church will be the cause of Satan's doom. In fact, it has always mystified me why Satan is still with us. If he's been tried and convicted and sentenced to the lake of fire, why is he still loose in this world?"

"Oh, I'm sorry I didn't make that clear, my dear. The trying and convicting, if you want to call it that, is what the Church is doing."

Veronica closed her eyes and shook her head.

"Isn't there enough evidence already?" Dr. Amill asked no one in particular.

"That would be heaven's call, not ours," answered Fr. Murphy.

"Evidence for what!" exclaimed Rev. Sweet. "Obviously that is what you two have never figured out. You need to ask the right question. There must be some argument Satan maintains that cannot be answered by all the evidence of all the evil he's sponsored in all the universe. What is it? If you don't know, then you must allow that Christ's reign on earth that you never took seriously might have something to do with answering Satan's plea. Getting out that answer, it seems quite clear to me, has to be the top of heaven's agenda, but it must be extremely involved."

"Who cares what Satan thinks?" grumbled Dr. Amill. "Evil has no claim to be treated with any kind of respect."

"I think you must know better than that about Satan," countered the priest. "Why shouldn't he have his day in court?"

"You two are trying my patience," said Veronica. "The only reason that Satan would still be with us is he hasn't had his day in court. Now tell me why that day hasn't come yet or stop wasting my time."

"What does St. Laura say?" asked the priest.

"Look, don't fool with me. I am not St. Laura's medium. But I think I'm seeing the answer. And if I know the answer, you can answer the question as well."

"If you know the answer, I believe you're ahead of all the doctors of Satanology. So I plead for enlightenment," said Fr. Murphy (and I suppose he winked at Dr. Amill).

"Satan has no plea whatsoever," declared Dr. Amill, "because God is ultimately responsible. Evil was necessary to develop good. Evil will come to an end exactly when God makes it end."

"Be careful there, Kirby," cautioned the priest. "Veronica won't stand for that. She's right: if our theology is worth anything we should know why Satan is still with us. If he has an argument with God, it shouldn't be a surprise. It wouldn't be the first time, as you well know. God pointed righteous Job out to Satan, and Satan disagreed, did he not? He maintained that none were beyond being tempted and said he could prove it. So God gave him permission to do so in order to settle the argument."

"All right, I'll give you a hint from the simple mind of Laura," said Veronica. "If Satan was created by God, he was created good, not evil. So where did the evil come from? Now I will add to that question what Dr. Amill said: Satan believes God is totally responsible for making him what he is."

"Okay, this is elementary, Veronica," said the priest. "We know how he got himself into trouble, do we not, Kirby? He got a bit prideful, and anyone might say rightfully so because he was a glorious being. But that bit of pride blossomed into opposition to his Creator. There was nothing in his being that prevented that. I call it free will. You may call it whatever you like, Kirby. Now God has to prove that free will does not inevitably lead to disobedience. But where is the evidence? All have sinned and fall short. Even Job was not perfect. So if God has mercy on human sinners, why not on devils? You see? It's a matter of justice! Have I answered the question, Rev. Sweet?"

"Justice was entirely satisfied by Christ on the cross," declared Dr. Amill before she could answer. "We became blameless in God's sight while Satan was destined to heap more guilt on his own head. And there you go. It's a simple case needing no trial."

"Put your feet where Satan's hoofs are for a second, Amill," continued Murphy. "Would you accept that as proof of anything? His point is that every one of us failed and deserved hell. The fact that humankind was rescued by God himself suffering for us proves that the defect had no cure. Or go back to the beginning: the fact that pristine, sinless Eve fell for Satan's argument proves volition's inherent weakness and tendency to sin."

"I would simply remind Satan that he never got Jesus Christ to step over the line," replied Dr. Amill. "There's ample proof right there that free will, if you want to call it that, does not have to lead to corruption."

"We're talking about *created* beings, Kirby," said Aaron. "The issue is that created beings, of which Satan is one, have all got this weakness, and we're all sinners as you say even from birth."

"You forget Satan is a spiritual being on the order of angels," countered Kirby. "He tried but was unable to get them all to follow him in opposing his maker. There's the simple proof that Satan cannot say his fall was inevitable."

"We have to assume that some of the angels were not in possession of the same order of volition," suggested the priest.

"That's a rather arbitrary assumption, is it not? And if that's the kind of reasoning you want to base your theory on, then I would advise you to save yourself the embarrassment."

At that point Veronica spoke up for clear-minded Laura. "No, Dr. Amill, it is not arbitrary unless you discount the strongest evidence the world has ever known apart from the fact that the whole creation itself groans for redemption. If a certain type of angel and the devil must have something in common with the human race in order to explain why certain humans were drafted this morning, then it must be so."

"You assume God's plan to deal with the devil hasn't been pursued until now," said Amill. "I see no basis for that assumption."

"Then are you going to tell us Satan has already been disposed of?" asked Fr. Murphy.

"No, not entirely. That awaits judgment day. But ever since Christ defeated death, Satan has been the toothless lion."

"Then why did Peter point to Satan's influence to explain why Ananias lied?" Fr. Murphy asked. "And why did Paul tell the Roman church that God would in the future bring about peace by bruising Satan under their feet?"

"I did not mean to imply that the effect was immediate."

"Why was it not immediate?" asked Veronica. "If he had been defeated, why was he still ruining lives?"

Dr. Amill shifted on his chair, and rather than answering Veronica directly he spoke to Fr. Murphy.

"Isn't it true that the lake of fire was prepared for Satan? That tells me that his doom is certain. Are you scholars saying the case will be reopened in order to give people an opportunity to accuse him before the court of heaven? If so, you will have to show me where that's written."

"Let me remind you," said Aaron, "that Satan does not necessarily agree with everything God says. God respects Satan's right to disagree; and when there is a disagreement there will be a test."

"And remind me what the disagreement between God and Satan is."

"That should be obvious to you, Kirby. Would you say that Satan had a free choice whether or not to obey God?"

"Yes, before he lost it he would have had a choice."

"How so?"

"By the power given him in his creation."

"Would it be unreasonable then for Satan to say that the power of free choice was an invitation to explore his options?"

"And that it was irresistible, I think you mean."

"That's precisely the point that has to be decided: whether or not free choice brings with it irresistible temptations."

"I don't see how human beings who have already followed Satan's example in disobeying God can stand as proof that perfect obedience is possible—if that's what you have in mind."

"Their slate has been wiped clean by the blood of Christ."

"And now because of that they will stand where Satan fell?"

"They have the benefit of remembering."

"Still, no man is perfect, and most are weak. Given enough time—"

"You mean the weakness will eventually activate the potential. I think that's true of most people. That's why a selection was made this morning."

"I believe it's possible," interjected Veronica, "and you would believe it too if you had known Laura."

Dr. Amill emitted a groan. "I suppose if you're going to redeem this earth, then some of its residents have to be incorruptible; otherwise the whole descent into rebellion and ruin could start over again. But that's a big *if* though I admit it's what the Old Testament looked forward to. Do you really think it's practical?"

"The New Testament says it too," said Aaron. "I'm reminded of Christ's letter to the church at Thyatira. At his coming he will give certain ones authority over the nations, to rule them with a rod of iron which has the ability to shatter them like clay pots. You get the picture that a few will rule the many with powerful tools."

"I'm looking that up to see exactly what it says," said Veronica as she worked with her phone. "Here it is: 'To the angel of the church at Thyatira write ...' and so on. Then it mentions Jezebel:

I cast her into a bed, and them that commit adultery with her into great tribulation, except they repent of her works.

"Isn't that interesting? It defines who goes through the great tribulation. Obviously not everyone does."

"Notice it says merely 'great tribulation,' not '*the* great tribulation,'" Dr. Amill pointed out. "There was sufficient tribulation in those early years to earn that title."

"Then explain the next verse," Veronica demanded.

And I will eliminate her children with death; and all the churches will know that I am he who searches souls and minds: and I will give to each one of you according to your works.

"These aren't martyrs," she pointed out. "They're eliminated in the great tribulation, and the churches understand why."

"It sounds awfully relevant, doesn't it?" Murphy put in. "It could be we missed the obvious interpretation, Kirby. Its easy to see now that there's no longer any reason to doubt the Rapture."

"It's very simple," Veronica stressed. "Once disobedience had corrupted creation, God set out to redeem everything. If he succeeds, the earth must produce good fruit, not bad fruit. Who is to say that humankind was not created in the image of God to facilitate the incarnation in order to produce witness against Satan after being inoculated against disobedience?"

"I see it clearly now!" exclaimed Fr. Murphy, "thanks to you and St. Laura. If the Millennium is the grand trial, then all that came before is preparation to produce a myriad of righteous, faithful, law-abiding, anointed, reborn, Spirit-infused, resurrected witnesses: from Adam to Noah to Abraham to Moses to David to Jesus as Servant to Jesus as King. And speaking of witnesses...."

Russell reappeared with disappointment written all over his face. "Prices have gone sky high," he said. "I can't find anything at less than twice yesterday's prices. I thought everything would be cheaper today. Now I'm thinking this wasn't such a good idea."

They to whom the good tidings were before preached
failed to enter in because of disobedience.
Hebrews 4:6

Chapter Eleven

Counting the Lost

*R*ussell Tarr is back at the hardware store along with
Simon, the only other member of the store's staff making
an appearance today. Not that the store was open on Sundays in
the past, but today is exceptional for several reasons.

Russell gave up his seat on the Rapture bus in order to keep
the store operating after the owners insisted they were abandoning it. Although he was unable to obtain a written note from
Philip Evans, he believes it was the Evans' intention to have him
take over the management if not the ownership. Philip knew that
Russell was on the fence and that if he had given him any indication that he could inherit the store, it would have persuaded Pastor Tarr to petition Jehovah to let him remain on earth—just to
make sure. As for Simon, the poor fellow never knew he needed to
absorb some wisdom from the Bible. Somehow he thought it was
optional, most likely having copied the attitude of like-minded
members of his church.

It appears now that all of the other former employees were
added to heaven's version of the church membership roll on the
last day new members were being accepted, and paradoxically,
Russell Tarr takes credit for that! He knows the gospel full well
and felt compelled to share it with them yesterday morning. He
was not sure until this morning whether he himself was in good
standing with heaven, but he has the consolation of always being
in good standing with Watchtower. He knew it was one or the
other, but he had not been able to renounce his claim to the credit
he had built up over the years and had decided he would let it ride
and see what happened—in case the Rapture did occur, which was
doubtful in the first place.

The Day and the Hour: Finally

So today Russell is assuming the role of owner and manager. He would like to close and lock the doors and spend the rest of the day putting in order what remains after the assault on the shelves that has taken place today. And though the "customer" traffic has lightened greatly, people are still coming in and ignoring him. The sign in the window instructs them to use the self-service check-out, but they are ignoring that too and walking out with whatever they like—in many cases with as much as they can carry.

Russell has been asked why he and Simon are still there. He wants to help the town get through the crisis, he says—by keeping the store in business. If there is any show of sympathy at that point, he goes on to make it known that he is looking for someone to run the office and take care of everything upstairs. They invariably seem to think that's funny, he said.

Simon has been trying to pick up after someone comes along the aisle in which he is working and sweeps items off the shelves. After he once received a kick and a threat, he no longer tries to stop them. Russell, working nearby, overheard Simon's complaint about the kick and demanded that the thief empty the sack and leave the store immediately. The response he got was not pretty. The man called him the "phony pastor left behind" and pulled a machete out of his sack, which was what he had threatened to do when Simon tried to stop him. Meanwhile, a man and his wife have come in and are carting away armloads of tools.

At the next lull in the traffic, Russell locks the doors and takes the sign out of the window, replacing it with a "Closed" sign, and turns off the lights. But repeat customers are already pounding on the door. Simon is scared and wants to leave by the back door. Russel is nervous and considers joining him, but he cannot quite let the remainder of the goods he considers to be his inheritance be stolen from him. What should he do? He knows about the instructions Jesus gave to his followers: give freely to anyone who asks. It appears that they may have to open it up and let the store be looted until nothing is left, but he is not quite ready to give up what he believes he has earned: he chooses to be its prisoner.

Counting the Lost

*K*aren came by and reported what she had found in the mine. I had brought Homer and Humphrey back with me, so you can imagine that Homer became very excited when he learned there is a way to get down to the level of the underside of the wreckage and possibly locate the spot where Earl Clark might be trapped.

Homer said he knows where he can get an inflatable kayak, and he is sure he will be able to get around handily down there with it. I told Karen I think most of that water had been in the mine a long time, and it might be several feet deep. If so, I reasoned that if Earl was on the ground floor when the building flattened and descended into the cavern, chances are his body is submerged. Homer and Karen both scolded me for bringing up the worst possible scenario. Homer pointed out that if Earl was in rising water, his survival might depend on getting to him immediately, which no one can deny. My hopes and prayers are that Earl Clark is alive and will be rescued, but also I have to be reasonable and not lead my readers to believe that he will show up later.

Karen had difficulty impressing on Homer how dangerous it is down there due to the risk of pieces of the wreckage breaking away and falling. Also dirt is still raining down. And at any time the great bulk of it might shift. From the noises she heard it seems likely to her that it *will* shift or even descend further. Homer was not intimidated. He still wanted to go immediately. Karen finally promised to go back tomorrow and see whether it had stabilized enough to make it safe to explore. It was not soon enough for Homer. He said he would go alone right now if she would let him have the key. Of course she would not hear of that.

Then Karen asked me if any of the abandoned vehicles had been removed from Beach House Road, to which I had no answer, so I called the towing company. I was told they can do nothing until they find their driver who has not responded to their calls and messages. On hearing this Homer offered to go help her move the cars. Karen agreed to this, and they left the dog with me.

The Day and the Hour: Finally

It was 4:30 when Jake came back. I've never seen him so dispirited. He confessed the futility of his refusing to allow the Rapture to be the Rapture, admitting that his holding out for it being an abduction by agents from another planet was absurd.[1] Now he wanted to discuss applied theology because, as he said in an exasperated tone, he had found no pattern in his observations.

By all accounts Felix had gone up with the chosen ones, which Jake could not reconcile with his concept of justice. He called Felix a moral monstrosity and questioned the wisdom of heaven for including him with the righteous.

Perhaps I am not the person to counter such an accusation. The best I could do was to point out that Felix had wrung more converts out of the town during the past week than had all the reputable professional preachers of the gospel put together.

Jake had inquired about that too, and he found evidence that a few of Felix's supposed converts had skipped the baptism and were not taken. He knew that baptism was regarded by some as conferring privilege, but even if that were true, how had Felix, who had been self-righteous to the point of total blindness, been able to convince so many to turn their backs to the world and embrace a promise from an ancient book. It was contrary to all reason that a man with a Pharisaical habit would be appealing to so many who despised the very hypocritical type he was.

I could think of no answer for Jake at that point that I thought would prove anything. In fact I had wondered the same thing. As you know, I sat in on Felix' lectures in which he plowed through the entire book of Romans—the apostle Paul's famous epistle to the church at Rome—and it occurred to me then that there could be significance in Felix's name being Paul Christian. So I mentioned this to Jake.

Jake is a practical man, and to him names are merely accidental; but that Felix would have the ability and inclination to lecture all the way through that book did mean something to him. Jake admitted that he had never read Romans himself.

---

1. The fine residual dust on the floor at Ned's house made an impression on him.

When he said that, I ventured to point out that we all are a little blind when it comes to judging the faults of others. I wasn't sure that Jake knew what Jesus said about that: that we can see a speck in the eye of another person and be unaware of something far larger in our own eye that distorts our judgment. So I didn't mention that. I just said that for some people there comes a time when things click into place, and they become like a new creature. I doubt that this satisfied him, but he changed the subject.

"What was the determining factor for rapturability?" he asked me. How would you answer that question? How could I speak with any conviction, let alone authority, for I had been wrong about the whole thing.

"It's the potential, not the present state of the person's soul that makes the difference," I said. I know, I had said nothing by that—intentionally—but Jake played along and tossed it back at me.

"What marks potential?" he asked.

"Faith. Childlike faith that leads to loving God and his Word."

"How is it then that every one of the Martin family is gone, including Hunter and Sookie. Sookie is the last person ...."

He stopped abruptly when I looked at him suspiciously.

"Felix got to her," I said.

"Then how did Felix get this transforming magic?"

"I don't know the full answer to that," I said. "But you know the pioneer prospector Joe Martin became a man of faith, and I daresay he prayed for his children. He might even have asked for the salvation of all his descendants. His son Ephraim went off to China as a missionary, and I happen to know—because I quizzed Felix on this—that an uncle of Felix's Chinese fiancé had in his possession a portion of Scripture with Ephraim Martin's name on it. Felix's fiancé was led to Christ by that uncle, and the news of her conversion galvanized Felix and turned him into an evangelist worthy of his name. So Sookie's salvation appears to be an answer to Joe Martin's prayer, and Felix was merely a link in a chain of events that reached one of the lost sheep in Joe Martin's family."

The Day and the Hour: Finally

Jake said he needed to think about that, and he left to go check on his survival camp over across the lake. Homer had gone to look for Asher who was not answering him, so I am left here alone and am about to do a little research of my own.

I have a list in front of me of people who are or were connected with Grace Bible Church whom I expect are still with us. Apparently only a small percentage of the townsfolk are missing, but the percentage is likely much higher among GBC members because their pastor was of that sort. I mean he was decidedly in the old-fashioned premillennial camp theologically, and he defended the Rapture doctrine more than anyone else. I was quite interested in what Adam preached because, frankly, there was a time a few years ago when I made an excursion into Protestant territory and became familiar with the dispensational approach. I will have to say that it integrates the Bible far better than amillennial interpretations do (which is of little concern if you are not a student of the Bible but only draw what you need from it as we normally do). So I tended to observe the members of that church, out of curiosity, to find out what practical difference their beliefs made in the way they saw fit to live. As you know, there are—or were—some outstanding disciples of our Lord among them, but there are—or perhaps were—others who did not impress me so much. I'm going to visit as many as I can find and have time to: first of all see if I'm right and secondly to learn how they are handling the disappointment (if it is a disappointment), which should be fascinating.

First on my list is Mary, who you may remember was protective of her daughter's Unitarian affiliation and requested that Wednesday's visitation team bypass her daughter's house for fear that they would incite the woman to anger if she suspected that her mother was behind the call. I know we can't reliably judge a person by such externals, but what do you think? I mean as a guess—before we find out. If Mary is home, will she have an excuse for being left behind? Or will she be relieved and be celebrating having escaped being an escapee. I suspect neither. ...

I did find Mary at home. She was surprised to see me, of course, but she did not ask why I was there. The television was on and showing some irrelevant thing, but she turned it off right away. When I mentioned the Rapture she dismissed it as though it were a rumor unworthy of her attention. She asked if I wanted a cup of coffee and then said she would have to borrow coffee from her daughter if I did. I hardly knew what to say that might connect with her concerns. I asked about her daughter, but she acted like she didn't hear me. *This is serious*, I thought.

"You're not far from the Federal Building here," I said. "Did it shake your house?"

"My house needs a new furnace," she responded. "Every winter it gets colder. Last winter Earl Clark came and cleaned it out. I'm going to call them tomorrow."

"Were you able to go to the concert at your church yesterday?"

"There wasn't any concert. Everything got called off. The doors were locked this morning, and the Murphy's weren't there."

"Did you go there, or did you hear that from someone?"

"Huh?"

"Did you go to the church this morning?"

"I don't know. I tried."

"Have you had anything to eat today, Mary?"

"Anything to eat? The TV has been on."

"Is there anything I can do for you?"

"What do you mean?"

"Do you need groceries?"

"No."

"Are you worried about something?"

"The furnace. I'm worried about the furnace."

"It's quite warm in here right now."

"Sometimes it gets too hot."

"Is there anything else that concerns you?"

"No."

"Would you mind if I ask someone from my church to visit you?" ...

The Day and the Hour: Finally

Well, you can imagine how it went. I saw no sign of intoxication; she was normal in her appearance. So I was puzzled because she was so different from what she had been last week. Finally I left her without making any meaningful connection. She was not utterly incompetent, so I judged that she would not harm herself. Tomorrow I will see if there is anyone at the hospital willing to evaluate her condition.

Now I'm inclined to go home and forget this project. But I think the chances are good that I've seen the worst and that the next person I find at home will lift my spirits a little.

Looking at my list, Connie is next. She lives—or lived—on this same street only two doors from Mary's house. Connie was not single, but her husband never went to church as far as I know. If anyone is home at least I'll find out if I'm right about Connie. She is an interesting case because there is so much of her on both sides of sanctity. She seems to know the Bible as well as anyone I've met, but she will never inherit the earth if meekness is the qualification. I think she would have become a more Christlike person if she had spent her life in the Catholic church, but no tickets to heaven on the Rapture train were handed out there. At least she had a chance where she was. If she is still with us, I expect a lively conversation. Hopefully it will make some sense. But why should I want her to be home? I need to confess something. Is it jealousy? ...

"Claudia! What are you doing here?" said Connie's husband as soon as he opened the door.

"Is your wife home?"

"Home. What do you mean home? Which home? She never knew which home she belonged to, this one or the one in the sky. But now she knows. I'm sorry. ... Connie! You have a visitor!"

Connie put on a good face, but she was not happy to see me, and I don't think she would have been happy to see anyone yet. The first thing she said was that she should have been a Catholic, which was amazing because it was what had crossed my mind minutes before. But I did not tell her that.

"I think your husband is a happy man today," I remarked. (We seemed to be alone, her husband having left as soon as she appeared.)

Connie didn't agree with me, but she didn't disagree either. I forget exactly how she said it, but I got the idea that church had been a refuge for her.

"Do you see Grace Bible Church coming through this?" I asked.

"No, I don't really," she said.

"Why don't you join us?"

"I might do that."

"Bring your husband too."

"Before I met him he was Catholic," she said.

"Perfect!" I said rather flippantly.

"No, I don't mean seriously, of course. We were right and you were wrong. So how can I switch to the wrong side? Out of spite? I'm not one known for her graces, but principles mean a lot to me."

"So where do we go from here, Connie? Some of our best leaders are gone."

"You don't mean in the city government, do you?"

"I believe some *are* gone. Does that surprise you? Apparently all levels were affected, but no official accounting has been done yet, of course."

"In fact it does surprise me," she said. "But you've not had enough time to determine that. Tomorrow you'll find very few absences after all, so I wouldn't worry about it."

"You know, getting a replacement for just one staff member even at the lowest level involves quite a process, and hiring a new janitor isn't much easier."

"You should order several artificial employees while you can get them," she advised me. "Keep them on standby until needed."

"They don't come cheap," I said. "The least expensive ones are made in China, but price is their only advantage except that they're multilingual. They understand Chinese ways better than our ways. To get a western-style one that's smart enough to be of any real help was beyond our budget capabilities when I looked into it a few weeks ago, and now with a likely reduction in tax revenue, I'm sure they're out of my reach. I wouldn't trust one anyway. You never know when software will get updated. It could be in the middle of a meeting, and then he, she, or whatever gender the thing is might quit working. If it's a full-body robot, and not just a talking head, you soon get mechanical failures, and you can't call the aid car or take him or her (or whatever the label says) up to the hospital; you have to wait for a technician to come out from the factory, which can take weeks. Then there's insurance, which is extremely expensive due to lawsuits brought against alleged physical and verbal abuse caused by software bugs which seldom can be reproduced. Also there's the droid union to contend with, which being run by artificially intelligent beings is unable to understand the human point of view on anything, and they go on strike every time an improved battery technology comes out until you update their contract and retrofit them with the latest type of battery."

"I don't believe it's that hopeless," said Connie, "but no doubt they are expensive. Your best option is to let the attrition be what it is. Consolidate positions and reduce services if necessary."

"Being employed by the FSA, your husband might be looking for other work, at least temporarily," I guessed.

"He said they made me stay behind so I could support him, but I don't know where he thinks I'll be able to get a job."

"If I have any openings that match your qualifications I'll let you know."

"Oh, he will find us some income somewhere. There will be openings at other FSA locations."

"Then you would have to move to another city."

"Yes, of course. I would prefer that, actually."

"You might find a suitable church."

"I'm through with church. Apparently I wasn't the kind of person Christ was interested in." ...

Counting the Lost

I left Connie shortly after that. She had not invited me, and I knew she was not enjoying our conversation, so I thanked her for sharing her thoughts, and she said it was quite all right.

Now the next one on my list is Doris. If you were at Grace Bible Church on that first Sunday evening, you will remember that she came in late. Not having heard the news of the Rapture dreams, she was shocked that people were saying the day and the hour had been revealed. She was unable to accept what was contrary to her firmly entrenched belief on that and soon left the meeting. As far as I know she did not attend any of the evening meetings after that.

Doris answered the door and seemed pleased to see me. ...

"I've been calling on a few people," I said, "because I wanted to get initial reactions to the culmination of that strange week."

"I ignored it," Doris said. "If anyone brought the subject up, I told them I didn't want to hear about it."

"Were you aware of what took place at the hospital?"

"I heard rumors. That's all they were. People make up stories to fit what they believe. I'm glad we're past the deadline. The whole thing will be quickly forgotten."

"Do you know of anyone who is missing?"

"No. No one's missing."

"I understand your pastor did not appear at his usual time."

"If he was late, I can understand that."

"Apparently he didn't show up at all, and the church remained locked."

"He was embarrassed, obviously. If he has to suffer a little bit for this, he deserves it."

"We know Pamela Evans disappeared because she was locked in Detention Suites."

"Do you really think she disappeared? No, that was a stunt. Why would she be in Detention Suites? Obviously that was a setup."

"Do you really think Pamela would participate in a setup to deceive people?"

"To save face people will lie and do almost anything."

"Jake has been around checking for evidence too. Brother Ned told Jake he saw his wife go, and Jake saw for himself a residue of fine dust which was all that was left of her."

"I wouldn't believe anything Brother Ned says. There's another case of someone trying to make it appear that the Rapture happened. I don't want to think about what he might have done with his wife."

"I was just over to see Connie before I came here. She believes the Rapture happened."

"She does?"

"I'm sure she does."

"Well, even Connie makes mistakes sometimes."

"I went to the Lakeview this morning to see how those folks were taking it, and the place was empty."

"That's not surprising. If Margaret was expecting the Rapture, she wouldn't have opened it."

"But I went in and saw evidence."

"You will see when everything comes out that it's been a hoax. Someone succeeded in making Bible-believing Christians look foolish, I'm sorry to say."

"How was it at the market this morning? Did you see anything that made you wonder?"

"I didn't go to work this morning. I had asked for the day off."

"Then you had no reason to not attend the morning service at GBC."

"I had intended to go, but I wasn't feeling well this morning. I watched "The Grace Bible Hour.""

"Which was recorded last week, wasn't it?"

"I suppose so, but there was nothing about the Rapture on the news channels. It's been forgotten already."

"Well, I'm glad you have gotten through this so easily. I'm having a great deal of difficulty." ...

That pretty well sums up what it was like with Doris. Such faith she has! It seems to me she should get a reward for that.

Help, Yahweh, for they have ceased being godly;
the faithful are no longer among the children of men.
Psalm 12:1

Chapter Twelve

Happy to be Left Behind

I had stopped by to see Sophie at her soap shop, and I was there but a short time when Geoffrey and his wife came in.[1] The four of us share a sort of camaraderie for having been present during most of Felix's lectures, in addition to being neighbors.

Geoffrey said they had been to Wendel's house and found evidence that made it look like he had been reduced to dust.

"We saw where he must have been sitting because his hearing aids were there by the chair, and there was this fine dust but no footprints anywhere," he said.

His wife proceeded to give the full account:

"We check on Wendel frequently since he lives alone and his health is poor. Usually he hears the doorbell, which is a loud buzzer. Since there was no answer to either the doorbell buzzer or when Geoffrey knocked repeatedly on the door—and I'm sure Wendel would have heard it even if he was not wearing his hearing aids because Geoffrey pushed the buzzer button several times and knocked so hard that the door rattled. Then finally he tried the door, and it was not locked. He called Wendel's name, and there was no answer. We didn't know if he was somewhere in the house—perhaps unconscious—or if he had gone out. We didn't think of the Rapture because nothing was said about it at Mass this morning. I noticed a strange smell in the house, and then Geoffrey noticed that everything was dusty. Even our shoes made marks on the floor, and there were no other footprints, so we knew Wendel had not been there. We thought he must have left, and then something had burned, but it wasn't ashes on the floor;

_____
1. I still do not know Geoffrey's wife's name. I was too embarrassed to ask and thought it would be mentioned.

it was like dust—like fine powder, but I have never seen anything like it. Then we saw his hearing aids on the floor near his easy chair—one of them was on the floor and the other one was on the chair. We didn't think he would have gone somewhere without his hearing aids. Geoffrey said that people sometimes catch fire and burn up, but there was no evidence of heat. It was spooky. I wouldn't go far from the door, but Geoffrey went and looked in every room. There was nothing unusual except the dust which was mostly in that one room, and more of it was closer to the chair. The smell was making me sick, so I went outside and waited for Geoffrey. He came out soon after I did. I said we should call the police. Geoffrey said he suspected it was the Rapture, and dust was all that was left of poor Wendel's body, probably because he was so frail he couldn't make it up into the clouds. When we saw your car, Claudia, parked in front of Sophie's shop, we thought you or Sophie might know what happened. We never once thought the Rapture had come because nothing was said this morning, and nothing was said about it on the TV news."

Sophie had been interested in what I had to share, and we had spoken briefly about some of the events of today that we knew about. So when Geoffrey and his wife came in I was able to confirm his conclusion and told him that the dust had nothing to do with Wendel's age.

"Dust to dust," I said. "God made Adam's body out of the dust of the earth, so when he unmakes a body that's all that's left."

"I hope it wasn't too painful," said Geoffrey's wife. "I'm glad we didn't go for it. It makes me more grateful than ever for the protection of the saints and the benefits of the rosary. What they got for defying the teaching of the Church doesn't seem like something God would do. The smell was revolting. I never thought Wendel would touch religion."

"Maybe he didn't," said Geoffrey. "Maybe it was extraterrestrials."

"If so then why wouldn't they take the body alive?" Sophie asked Geoffrey.

"Well, they did. They packed him in some kind of dust that puts the body in a state of hibernation."

"Then they carried him out to their space vehicle parked in the street while you were at your church his morning. Or are they able to make themselves invisible?" Sophie retorted.

"Do you have a better explanation?"

"It was a miracle, Geoffrey," I said.

"I don't believe God would turn an old man into dust," insisted Geoffrey's wife. "If you told me it was done by a wicked witch, I might believe you, but God doesn't do things like that."

"According to your Bible he nuked Sodom," said Sophie.

"And Lot's wife got turned into salt, as I recall," I said.

"That's the Old Testament, isn't it?" said Geoffrey with a grin.

"Yes, it is," I said.

"We don't have to believe everything in the Old Testament, do we?" Geoffrey asked. The man was laughing inside, I'm sure.

"Geoffrey knows more about the Bible than he pretends to know," said his wife. "But we don't focus on that so much. The best things are in the monthly newsletter Father Murphy sends out. He makes sure we dwell on the most helpful things from the Bible."

"What time is it?" Geoffrey asked rhetorically. "Four o'clock. I don't want to miss ..."

"You're welcome to leave any time," said Sophie.

And they did leave immediately. I wanted to say something to soften the atmosphere before they left, but I let it go. I must admit I'm not feeling charitable today.

"I can't stand that man's wife," said Sophie as soon as the door closed behind them.

As I had no reply forthcoming, she must have assumed I felt the same way because she launched into a tirade against her. I will not repeat it (in fact I could not repeat it) nor will I try to summarize it, only to say I can glean no virtue from it worth repeating. I was looking on Sophie's chart of enlightenment on her wall and vainly trying to fit her speech in there somewhere. ...

The Day and the Hour: Finally

The next one on my list is Lucinda. She is one of those rare persons who waits her turn to speak and then speaks her mind without calculating how it may affect her reputation. If she avoids being offensive, it is for other reasons—genuine concern for the feelings of others, I think. She attended (by accident) a meeting of my Catholic friends and I where Lazar MacDonald presented his novel vision of purgatory, and during the debate afterwards, in which the institutional authority of the Church was mentioned, she brought up a very pertinent question about the identity of the Nicolaitans—a question she had gotten from Adam Murphy's sermon. With so much in her favor, the only reason I wonder whether she is still with us is the fact that she freely admitted her objection to the Rapture coming along and interrupting her life. ...

I did find her home, and she seemed happy to see me. I had a very positive talk with her.

"You don't seem to be disappointed," I said.

"No. I'm relieved. It isn't that I was completely unwilling to embrace the benefit of moving to heaven, it's just that I never understood why life should be interrupted. I believe everything is orchestrated in detail by God, and one moment becomes the next by the wisdom of the ages. So why this discontinuity? It didn't feel right, and if it felt right to others, they were way beyond me. So in my spiritual immaturity, if that's what it is, I'm here to do my part and carry on with the responsibilities of normal life."

"If everyone was as honest as you are, there would have been more objections to an interruption of normal life," I said. "It's one thing to read about it in a fantasy novel or see it depicted in a cin-ematic thriller, and it's quite something else to face it in real life. That's why I think there was never supposed to be a warning. But on the other hand, the warning made it a test of faith not unlike what the martyrs faced when they were put to death."

"Yes, if you're about to be killed by men, you know God is on your side, but it doesn't feel right to me to have God being the one causing your exit, and yet you're supposed to think of it as a good thing. Well, maybe for someone who's very unhappy it would be."

"What interests me is that you're still here while others are gone who undoubtedly were as unwilling as you are, only they were afraid to say so."

"Perhaps they never asked their Father in heaven to excuse them from the draft."

"Like conscientious objectors?"

"Something like that."

"And you did?"

"Yes, I did."

"Then that would explain why Kirby Amill and his congregation all got left behind. They objected to the premillennial doctrine, which was the same as requesting that it not apply to them."

"And it was your request to be left behind too?" she asked me.

What could I say? "Yes, the same default prayer would have to be mine and every Rapture-despising member of my church."

"I see the wisdom of the warning," said Lucinda in her guileless way. "It presented you all an opportunity that was backed up by an obvious miracle."

"Yes, I see what you're getting at. But tell me plainly—an opportunity for what?"

"To serve in the Millennium."

"So this was like being drafted into an army?"

"Exactly like that."

"In the case of a military draft, I can understand that the army prefers willing servants if it can get them," I said. "Or at least if they say they're willing, then they have more potential as fighters. But being called to heaven isn't like being called to war."

"It *is* being called to war," said Lucinda, and she laughed. "That's what the Rapture was for, which is the main reason I didn't like it. I must admit I'm not as honest as you thought I was."

"Well, I'll give you credit for admitting it."

"What choice did I have? I had gotten myself into a corner with no other way out."

"I'll take some of the blame for getting you there. I'm glad you're here, and I'm glad we're in this together." ...

The Day and the Hour: Finally

Finally, I thought I should check on Maud. She is my neighbor, after all, and I expect we will be neighbors for some time. Why do I sound confident about that? I know Adam Murphy was concerned about her, for one thing. She was one who spoke out at the evening meeting last Sunday, expressing her desire to be left behind, and she wanted to know if putting in a request for it would be allowed. Perhaps because of that, her pastor called on her on Friday. Though Maud was a longtime attendee at GBC, he found her disbelieving if not ignorant of the gospel. Another reason I think I will find her at home is that she has a reputation for being unforgiving about an event in the past. I take it that Jesus meant it when he said, "If you forgive others their trespasses, your heavenly Father will also forgive you, but if you do not forgive others their trespasses, neither will your Father forgive your trespasses." ...

The doorbell was answered by Digby, Maud's live-in companion and helper. Yes, Maud is home, he said, and he went to warn her that I was wanting to speak with her. I stood there in the entry for perhaps five minutes. I suppose some hasty housekeeping was taking place, as the strong odor was not what you generally find in a well-kept residence.

When I was finally ushered into her presence, her little dog gave out a sharp "yap," which did not sound friendly, and Maud's countenance as she sat with the dog on her lap was not welcoming either. I thought she might be in a bad mood because of the Rapture, so I avoided the subject and asked after her health because she appeared to be living on her couch. She said she had lost her health when she and her late husband endured terrible mistreatment from the city building department. This was before my time, which she acknowledged, but she proceeded to tell me her side of the story and complain that I managed to get extensive renovations approved for my place which she said were not allowed to her husband and which led to his early death and her chronic illness. I believe there is some truth in that. From the other side I had heard that her husband was extremely difficult to deal with and would not accept compromises. It was his own way or nothing.

I mentioned to Maud that forgiveness was enjoined by Jesus, and it promoted healing in body and soul. Her response was that the matter needed to be set right before she could forgive the city. I pointed out that the building-department employees whom her husband had differences with were no longer there, but that made no difference in her mind. She wanted justice done and demanded a reimbursement for the funds they spent on materials and labor for a wall that had to be taken down and for the fines that were unjustly levied. I told her I did not have the authority to do that on my own, which she said she understood, but she was going ahead with a new lawsuit against the city, nevertheless.

"Why now?" I asked her.

"Because I'm through being a member of Grace Bible Church in good standing. There are people there who work for the city, and they have been leaving me alone, so I didn't want to make more enemies."

I thought she was alluding to the closure of Grace Bible Church, but she went on to tell me she had joined the Mormon Church. She made no reference to the Rapture, so I was beginning to suspect that she did not know it had happened. She went on to describe the wonderful service she had attended this morning and the kindness of the people there.

Finally I could contain my curiosity no longer, and I asked her if she was aware that many people had left Grace Bible Church and I thought it would probably be closed for the foreseeable future. She asked where they had gone.

"To heaven," I said.

She stared at me in disbelief as if I were making a joke, and then it seemed she remembered the Rapture.

"There was no mention of anyone disappearing this morning," she said.

"I'm not surprised. No Mormons had the dream."

"Then it must be of the devil," said Maud. ...

The Day and the Hour: Finally

That was my last visit and what I thought was the end of my research for today. When I got back to the house I found Homer waiting for me. The reality of losing his best friend, Asher Cypher, and his girlfriend, Victoria Martin, in addition to his hero, Earl Clark, had begun to sink in. He was one dejected young man.

"How much of the team is left?" I asked him.

"They're all here. All but Asher. But without Mr. Clark there's no team. ... Did you know this would happen?"

"No, but I was afraid it would. I thought you would go with your family if it did. Would you rather have gone with them?"

Homer had difficulty answering that. He said he did not know.

"I know the team rule is what got you into the Church. But you had no objection to converting, as I remember."

"My mother told me once she was happier when she was a Catholic. I don't understand why she was taken. She wasn't very sincere. I could mention a lot of things, but I won't."

"So you thought if you were left behind she would be too?"

"Probably."

"I agree it's very confusing, and it doesn't seem fair. You can stay with me for awhile at least. No one is using the guest house."

"Is Jake here?" Homer asked.

"Jake left to go to his camp across the lake."

"Why?"

"To see that it's ready for a long-term stay if he needs it."

"What does he think will happen?"

"He thinks because key people are gone there'll be trouble."

"Trouble—like what?"

"Well, he's in the real estate business. All of a sudden there's a surplus of houses without owners. That means trouble for banks and courts as well as law enforcement, and key people are probably missing in all of those agencies. Jake thinks there will be auctions at rock bottom prices, which is not good for his business."

"Maybe I could get a house to live in."

"You have a house, don't you?"

"My parents did, but I don't want to live there anymore."

184

Happy to be Left Behind

I was showing Homer the guest house when my phone announced that I had a visitor. Alex Smart was at the front door. I asked him to wait a minute. I told Homer to make himself comfortable while I attended to the visitor. Homer wanted to know if Humphrey must stay out; I gave him permission to let the dog in.

Alex said he was looking for a job. He said the newspaper is out of business because both Chester and Earl are gone, which means a smaller local market for the products of the recycling mill he manages. It was barely scraping by before this happened, and he doubts that further subsidies will be forthcoming.

I asked him about his qualifications and if he had any experience in government work.

"Much of my work in the Navy was administrative," he said. "Being in command of a fleet entails much more than giving out sailing orders. It requires a lot of skill and the ability to make good decisions quickly. I commanded hundreds of people in the course of my career, and I became expert at selecting people to fit positions. Everything had to be done with an eye on the budget, of course, and when overruns were unavoidable I always succeeded in finding creative ways to get the job done. One must be studious about every aspect of your organization, you know. You not only have to know how it works, or is supposed to work, you have to know how to fix it where it's broken. When I took over the recycling mill they were bogged down with all kinds of technical problems and were in danger of having the startup funding canceled. I immediately attacked the problems, one by one, and got the project back on track. By the end of the first year I was there it was running smoothly and generating profit from product. Now with that much successful administrative experience, I have no doubt that I could help you deal with any problems that may be coming up as a result of the loss of your key personnel. You will find that I'm worth two or three of your average government professionals, and you won't have to worry about mistakes or overspending. I'm quite familiar with the workings of city governments, as it has been a primary interest of mine."

The Day and the Hour: Finally

I told RADM Smart I had never encountered an overqualified person in city government, and so I assumed it was not a good thing, but that I would think about it and let him know.

Then it occurred to me that Homer was most likely hungry, whether or not he had eaten anything today. As I started back to the guest house to ask him about that, I remembered that Sookie was missing—in fact all the Martins were missing—and the Green Broccoli would be needing someone to look after the machines and wait on customers. Perhaps Homer could help me with that in trade for his room.

Homer agreed, and we went down to open it for dinner.

While we were there, Rand[1] came in expecting to get a meal, apparently. (Since the Lakeview is out of business at least temporarily I think the Broccoli will be doing much better.) But Rand had another matter on his mind as well.

"I'm not working right now," he said, "and so I would like to offer my services to the city."

"Since when are you not working?" I asked.

"My contract ended last week."

"And what kind of service do you have to offer? You used to travel a lot. Have you observed something done differently elsewhere you want to implement here? By the way, you attended Grace Bible Church when you were in town, isn't that right?"

"So you're asking what's my excuse for being here?"

"Do you have one?"

"I used to have one. You might say it became obsolete this morning, but I still stand by it. It makes no sense to disrupt the economy of the world before the Tribulation begins. A lot of key people are AWOL, and that means businesses will shut down or be crippled and people will be laid off. So I don't mind not contributing to that."

"All right, Rand. What is your proposal?"

"To take a census for the city—or maybe all of Sorek Valley."

---

1. You may remember Rand from the episode on Tuesday evening when he presented his pretribulation Rapture denial to Harold and Philip.

> God put in their [the rulers] hearts ... to come to one mind, and to give
> their kingdom to the beast until the words of God should be accomplished.
> Revelation 17:17

Chapter Thirteen

No End in Sight

*L*ate this evening I received a phone call from Larry Link in Babylon. You may have wondered how I knew about Lucy. Not only was Larry grieving over his loss and his foolishness, he was homesick already. He talked and talked. I wrote those two sketches about him and Lucy from what he told me this evening and inserted them in the chapters chronologically. But there is more that I think will interest you.

Larry told me that he and Larry Jr. went out as soon as it was light, which was 7:00 Monday morning there, 8:00 tonight here. They found a dog-friendly food bar where they took some breakfast and then set out walking along one of the canals. He thought he would try to enjoy what he could of the Great City, but his thoughts were about Lucy and he could not enjoy himself.

Along the way he paused for a man who took a liking to Larry Jr. It occurred to Larry, as he looked down at the two of them going through the stroking and sniffing ritual—which is the same in every country and language worldwide—to inquire if anything had been revealed yet about the antichrist. Since the man made no immediate reply, Larry assumed he knew little English. He had said something about liking the dog in English, but in his conversation with Larry Jr. he spoke a tongue Larry did not recognize. In another attempt to get a response, Larry added that he knew a little about the council of seven headed by Sunday.[1]

The man stood up and laughed. He told Larry in good English that there were many rumors about the resurrection of Babylon.

---

1. Somehow Larry had heard about Sunday and his committee last week. I had gotten my information through Ahuva when she was working for me in the Gallery, so Larry could have heard about it from her. Either that or he got it from Willard MacDonald who printed some early versions of this chronicle. Apparently nothing happens that Larry does not hear about.

The Day and the Hour: Finally

When Larry expressed an interest in hearing more, the man told him things that Larry knew I would be interested in, which is why he called me.

Larry said his friend told him that Sunday was only remotely responsible for the development of the Great City, but that it was on the morning news that he had been confirmed as the Antichrist by someone higher—someone or something from whom he takes his orders.

"Isn't the Antichrist supposed to step in and run the world?" Larry asked the man.

"That's true, and it isn't. Do you know who Sunday's boss is?"

"I thought he was the kingpin behind all the kingpins," said Larry.

"Have you heard of the Beast? Sunday's boss is a Uninet robot! The Beast kept expanding and adding to its knowledge base and exponentially growing its intelligence, so by now it knows everything and has the intelligence to apply it. The thing was programmed to take advantage of every opportunity to insert itself into information streams to monitor and ultimately take control. So it has been doing that, and now there is no way to stop it."

"Will they have to shut down the whole Uninet to kill it?" Larry asked the man who seemed to know everything himself.

"No one will do that because the Beast knows too much. Whenever a hacker tries to disable it, the Beast pushes information onto the hacker that gives him the ability to blackmail important people and also lets the important people know who has the goods on them. And you know what happens next."

"The hacker finds himself dead," Larry supposed.

"That's right. You don't live long after you oppose the Beast."

How much of this is true, I don't know. It doesn't conflict with the information I had gotten ostensibly directly from Saturday who had been a member of Sunday's committee. I had Sunday making veiled reference to a power that wielded authority over him, but I assumed the connection was purely spiritual. Has the devil taken over the Uninet? Or is this material evolution?

I wonder about Enid and Ernie. On the news there was a report of a cruise ship going on the rocks. I think it was the one they were on. When I get more details, I'll go back and add them into the story.

I'm going to wind this up for the time being. I want to interview Soren and Sylvia Foster, if they're still here, because I need a bookend that goes with the Prologue. And that will be it for now.

When I went to the other Foster household to get Harrietta's painting, I was prepared to find her still there, but I was wrong. I found Homer instead. I've been wrong about several things today. It feels like we've entered a new era of unpredictability. Maybe it's just the lingering trauma of the FSA building collapse.

I'm tempted to say something about Harrietta that would not be kind—whether it would be a criticism of her or God's sense of justice, I'm not sure. Grace is fine, but it has limits. I thought it did, anyway. I'm not sure of anything anymore.

The painting was there, but I haven't taken it yet. I'll get it tomorrow perhaps. I don't know what I'll do with it.

Homer still has hopes of finding Earl alive and rescuing him. He says Karen Martin is willing to take him down into the mine tomorrow. I've cautioned her against that, but she is as determined to find Earl—or his remains—as Homer is.

I could use Homer at the Broccoli, and he could stay here, but he says he wants to work full time for the Lord to honor his father. He wants to reopen Grace Bible Church. I can't blame him for being disillusioned with my church. He doesn't appear to be holding it against me, but in a way I wish he would because I know I'm guilty of severing him from his family even if he doesn't think so. He considers Earl Clark the only family he has left. If Earl is no longer with us, he doesn't want to play baseball anymore.

The town will not be the same without Earl. We all miss him terribly and will miss his helping hand in the days to come if he doesn't emerge from that dreadful grave alive. Either way I'll never speak to Al Cypher again.

The Day and the Hour: Finally

Soren and Sylvia Foster spent a restful morning at home as was their habit. Occasionally they would attend the Sunday-morning church service when not traveling, but more often they spent the entire Lord's day at home, taking it easy.

Soren awoke a little earlier than usual and spent an hour swimming in the indoor pool. When eight o'clock came he was in the kitchen making poached eggs and toast for himself. The brief jolt of an earthquake caused the floating eggs to sway in the pan, but since the kitchen did not look toward the lake he did not see the choppy little waves. Earthquakes are not rare; he braced for the typical series of shocks to follow and thought it odd that there were none. After waiting a few moments, he resumed his breakfast preparation. The house was constructed to withstand earthquakes, and he was not concerned about damage.

Sylvia, having enjoyed a leisurely bath, found Soren in the kitchen finishing his second slice of gluten-free bread smothered under marmalade.

"Did you feel an earthquake?" she asked him.

"I surely did. It was a strange one. But I'll take a brief thing like that over a normal tremor."

"I was getting out of the tub and almost fell. At first I thought it was my own unsteadiness, but if you felt it too, I think I'm all right. What time is it?"

"8:15."

"Pastor Murphy's Rapture was supposed to happen at eight o'clock. You don't suppose there was something to it after all?"

"I had completely forgotten about it," Soren admitted. "The quake might have been at exactly eight o'clock. If so, Murphy will have something to his credit. That would be remarkable indeed."

"The Rapture was supposed to be worldwide. Could the earthquake have been felt around the world?"

"No, that's not possible. I reckon it was a rare coincidence that we got a quake near the time they were all supposed to leave the earth."

No End in Sight

It was mid-morning when Soren settled into his chair in the reading room with easy-listening music playing. Sunday was a day to be detached from the world and its troubles. As a rule they abstained from the Uninet. Neither did they check email, and they seldom answered a phone call. This practice made Sunday very special, a day protected, anticipated, and one which the doctor relished after a career of answering emergency calls every day of the week.

Suddenly the music was interrupted by things rattling on the shelf and a distant yet detailed sound of twisting steel and cracking concrete. Soren waited, trying to think what it might be. When the second noise came he got up and went outside. He observed a plume of dust billowing about the place where the top of the Federal Building had formerly been clearly visible above the trees. Sylvia came out to join him, and he pointed it out to her.

"It must have been weakened by the earthquake," said Soren. "Few people really trusted that building. It wasn't designed right. Well, I always said it was too big for this town anyway. I don't think we'll miss it, really."

"I hope no one was inside it when it fell," said Sylvia.

"Good thing it's Sunday. There wouldn't have been many—hopefully none," said the doctor.

"There might have been prisoners in the Detention Center," Sylvia pointed out. "Is there anything you can do to help them?"

"I think there are people on duty for emergencies."

The sound of screaming sirens began confirming his statement.

"Let's go back inside where it's quiet," he suggested.

Returning to his chair, he picked up the book that waited on chair-side table. It was C. S. Lewis' *The Great Divorce*. He had started it the night before.

At one o'clock Sylvia entered the room. She had been tending to things in her greenhouse.

"In case you're interested, I have made a little lunch for us," she announced.

Soren demonstrated his interest by following her to the nook near the kitchen, where windows overlooked a garden and a table was set with crackers, cheese, and cold salmon.

"You have really gotten into your book today," she judged from his silent mood.

"It's a strange little book. A psychological fantasy, I would call it. Various characters are given the chance to escape hell and go to heaven if they will give up their own petty peeves and grudges and ambitions, which, of course, are incompatible with heaven. But so far they've all been turning away from the very entrance to paradise, preferring their own ways even if it means living in ultimate impoverishment. Each one was met by a caring and significant person who offered specific and appropriate assistance, beseeching and imploring the poor soul to take even the first step toward the light of freedom and release from bondage. But with one exception they chose to return to the dim regions of the underworld, which are familiar if not comfortable. It's delightfully written in the first person, and so far it rings true."

The afternoon slipped away quietly at the Soren Foster household. The doctor spent the whole time reading the book.

Evening shadows have now faded into twilight, and the gloom of a cloudy night overshadows the town. Sylvia comes in to join him, with a book in her hand. The smart lights in the ceiling follow her across the room as if she were a performer on a stage. She takes her place in the other easy chair and begins reading.

Soren has nearly finished *The Great Divorce*. He has gotten to the most profound discussion in the story, where George MacDonald appears as a character, trying to impart to Lewis (and the reader) a deeper understanding of destiny, when Sylvia interrupts him. Just then the lights go out followed by the sound of their emergency generator starting, and presently the lights come on.

"Soren, look at this book," Sylvia says excitedly. "It seems to be alluding to the Rapture. It has the whole Martin family leaving us! Or am I reading something into it that isn't there?"

"Where did you get it?"

"I picked it up at the craft fair yesterday. Willard MacDonald had it in his booth. This was his only copy. He said it was the first copy of the complete story, whatever that means. It was nice of him to let me borrow it."

"Okay, let me see. ... Hmm—*The Day and The Hour*."

"It's a story book. I opened it to the end to see if it said anything about the author and discovered this history of the Martin family. I've always thought someone should write a history of the Foster family; that's why I was interested in it. Not many people are aware that Garrett Foster raised the money to build the hospital."

"That's true. It was perfect timing for Becher. But then, Becher's graduation from medical school was perfect timing for my father since the town was short of doctors, and he was being severely overworked."

"Check out the genealogy," Sylvia urged.

The Martin family:

Joseph 1870 - 1955
    Manasseh 1899 - 1915
    Ephraim 1900 - 1962
        Becher 1935 - 1992
            Kenneth 1960 -
                Hunter 1979 -
                    Sookie 2000 -
                Kevin 1983 -
            Luke 1965 -
                Timothy 1988 -
                    Victoria 2007 -
                Tabitha 1990 -
            Deborah 1967 -

"Hmm. When was this printed? ... This year. I don't recognize the author. It had to be some member of the Martin family. Hmm. I think it must have been written by Hunter."

"You don't say."

The Day and the Hour: Finally

That's probably it. Those FSA employees have easy jobs with lots of spare time on their hands, which allows them to get into all kinds of mischief."

"Soren, your theory is ridiculous: it was written by a woman."

"That name doesn't mean much. It could have been written by anyone."

"Did you see the chronology on the next page?"

"No. ... Oh, yes; here it is."

Martin Family Chronology:

1870   Joseph Kenneth Martin born

    1889   discovers gold.

    1890   stakes claims 1891 - Claims bought by John Howard

    1891   buys land at north end of lake

    1892   leaves town

        1892   Port Townsend - invests in building

        1894   bankrupt - Shanghaied

        1895   Shanghai - meets Hudson Taylor - becomes Christian

        1897   Port Townsend - fishing

        1898   marries Asenath, American Indian

1898   Joseph returns

        builds cabin near present site of Beach House

1899   Manasseh Martin born to Joseph and Asenath

1900   Ephraim Martin born to Joseph and Asenath

1912   Ephraim preaches his first sermon

1915   Manasseh Martin dies in mine accident

1920   Ephraim builds church on Ridge Ave

1930   Ephraim and Joe build Beach House - Joseph remains in cabin

1931   Ephraim marries Martha Howard

1935   Becher Martin born to Ephraim and Martha

1940   Ephraim and Martha go to China as missionaries with CIM

1940   Joseph and Asenath move into Beach House with Becher

1953   Becher leaves for college

1955   Joseph Martin dies

1957	Becher marries Beverly Stern
1960	Kenneth born to Becher and Brenda
1961	Becher returns from college
	moves into Beach House, works at hospital
1962	Ephraim Martin dies in Shanghai
1965	Luke born to Becher and Brenda
1967	Deborah born to Becher and Brenda
1979	Kenneth marries Cynthia MacDonald
1979	Hunter born to Kenneth and Cynthia
1980	Kenneth moves to Boise with family
1983	Kevin born to Kenneth and Cynthia
1983	Luke leaves for college
1987	Luke marries Lily Anderson
1988	Timothy born to Luke and Lily
1992	Becher Martin dies
1992	Kenneth, divorced, returns with Hunter
	(Kevin remains with mother in Boise)
1992	Kenneth and Hunter move into Beach House
1992	Luke back from college
	joins Kenneth in Beach House, works at hospital
1993	Kenneth builds house uptown for Luke
1995	Kenneth builds house on lake for self
1999	Hunter marries Hilda Harrison
2000	Sookie Martin born to Hunter and Hilda
2005	Kenneth marries Karen Baker
2006	Timothy marries Vivian Torres
2007	Victoria Martin born to Timothy and Vivian in Herne
____	Kenneth, Luke, Lily, Hunter, Hilda, Sookie leave town suddenly

"Hmm. I see what you mean."

"Could it be prophetic?" she asks.

"It doesn't say anything about a Rapture event, if that's what you mean. No, I don't think it means that. Hmm—'leave town suddenly'—extremely vague. I don't think we can deduce anything from it. They're not all supposed to leave town suddenly are they? I mean it's only for believers, isn't it? Anyway, Kevin isn't listed."

"He still lives in Boise, doesn't he?"

"As far as I know he does. Well, Luke's sister isn't listed either."

"Deborah lives in the city and so does Tabitha."

"That leaves Timothy and Victoria who live in Herne, I believe."

"That's right."

"Oh, here's a history of residency at the Beach House."

Beach House history:

1929-1930	built by Joseph and Ephraim Martin
1930-1940	Ephraim Martin
1940-1955	Joe Martin
1955-1961	Homer Foster
1961-1992	Becher Martin
1992-1995	Kenneth Martin
1995-1997	Harold Foster
1997-1998	vacant
1998-2007	Philip Evans
2007-2008	vacant
2008-	Kenneth Clark

"I see an error here," declares the doctor. "They show Earl Clark's first name as 'Kenneth.' Whoever wrote this must not have first-hand information to make an error like that."

"Why don't you call Luke? If he answers his phone, we'll know for sure there was nothing to the Rapture scare. I'm sure he will answer when he sees it's from you."

"All right. ... He's not answering. ...

"Luke, just checking to see whether you know anything about the Federal Building. It appears to have collapsed. Please give me a call when you get a chance.

"He must be indisposed right now. He'll call back soon. Let's check the news. I have a feeling something *is* going on."

As reported earlier, the government of Israel has been cooperating with UN peacekeeping forces to protect Jews from persecution by relocating them to the International Compound for Endangered Jews located at Bozrah, Jordan. This will not only conserve the lives of vulnerable Jews, but it is the final solution that will allow peace in Palestine. The UN has the support of the Vatican and the World Council of Churches in this. Elsewhere, Jews are being detained for their protection as well. Peace is at hand.

There has been an interruption of the pattern of the mysterious TV signals supposedly being received from outer space. At eleven o'clock, Eastern time, the messages from the New Testament disappeared and were replaced by a steady message from the Old Testament: the single verse Hosea 5:15.

There are conflicting reports about the so-called Rapture. There are no known genuine video recordings of people disappearing. Hundreds of spoofs have appeared on BooTube, but nothing that has been authenticated. Church attendance this morning was lower than usual, though many smaller churches were closed. There are reports of missing persons, however. The whereabouts of the President is unknown at this time.

Security alerts are out for communities near penitentiaries. There have been escapes, possibly due to earthquake damage.

Some of the parties that were planned to celebrate the Rapture are going ahead despite the uncertainties.

The picture switches to a ballroom in a hotel showing partiers sitting in chairs, drinking and watching the news.

"Soren?"

"What is it?"

"We're in this book."

"That's a good one, dear. You mean it's a story about a doctor and his wife?"

"No. The first chapter starts out describing our town to a *T*. I wouldn't be surprised to find our names in it."

The ceiling lights flicker.

"Is something wrong with the generator, Soren?"

"It must be out of fuel. I forgot to order diesel oil to replace what we used during that long outage last winter."

The generator stops, and the lights go out.

The Day and the Hour: Finally

Street Map

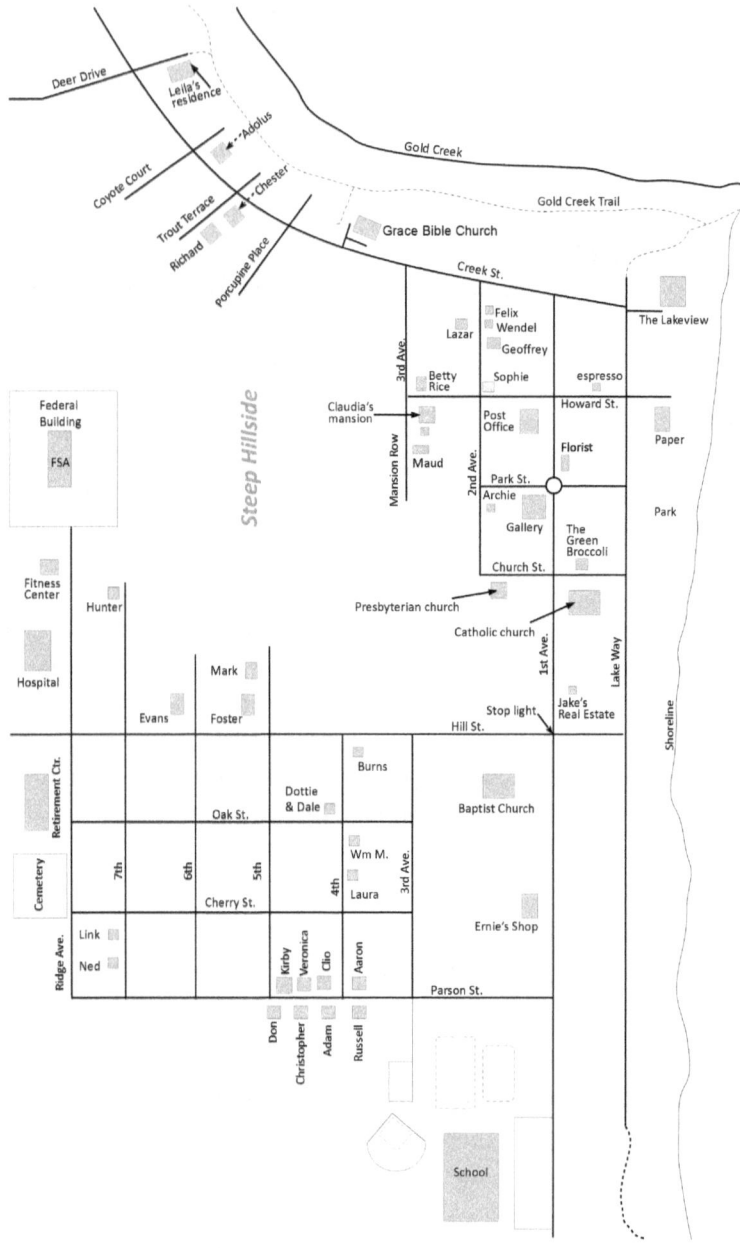

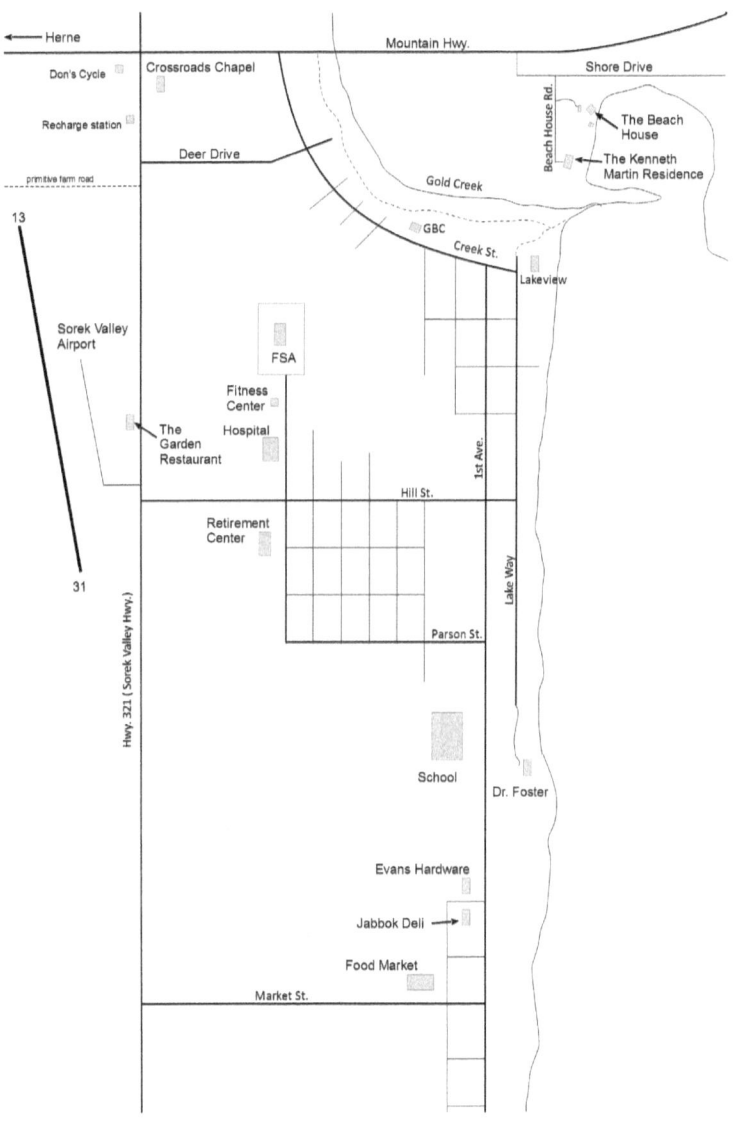

The Day and The Hour

Continued in *The Days Afterward*

For information about books by Lynn Andrew, visit
www.dayandhour.com